Brian P. Murphy

At the bar, Mucker started to grin
broadly as he watched the knife appear in
Verde's left hand. He darted a delighted
glance at Halford, but it was not
returned. Equally aware of what was
going on, the big man began to lift
his rifle with the right hand so he
would be ready in case something went
wrong and Verde failed to do his work.
Young Ole Devil Hardin had walked
into a trap and it was about to be
sprung on him . . .

List of J. T. Edson titles in chronological order

THE HARD RIDERS
THE FLOATING OUTFIT
APACHE RAMPAGE
THE RIO HONDO WAR
THE MAN FROM TEXAS
GUNSMOKE THUNDER
THE SMALL TEXAN
THE TOWN TAMERS
RETURN TO BACKSIGHT
TERROR VALLEY
GUNS IN THE NIGHT

Waco series
SAGEBRUSH SLEUTH
ARIZONA RANGER
WACO RIDES IN
THE DRIFTER
DOC LEROY, M.D.
HOUND DOG MAN

Calamity Jane series
CALAMITY, MARK AND
  BELLE
COLD DECK, HOT LEAD
THE BULL WHIP BREED
TROUBLE TRAIL
THE COW THIEVES
CALAMITY SPELLS
  TROUBLE
WHITE STALLION, RED
  MARE
THE REMITTANCE KID
THE WHIP AND THE
  WAR LANCE
THE BIG HUNT

Alvin Dustine 'Cap' Fog series
YOU'RE A TEXAS
  RANGER, ALVIN FOG
RAPIDO CLINT
THE JUSTICE OF
  COMPANY 'Z'

'CAP' FOG, TEXAS
  RANGER, MEET MR.
  J. G. REEDER

The Rockabye County series
THE SIXTEEN DOLLAR
  SHOOTER
THE SHERIFF OF
  ROCKABYE COUNTY
THE PROFESSIONAL
  KILLERS
THE ¼ SECOND DRAW
THE DEPUTIES
POINT OF CONTACT
THE OWLHOOT
RUN FOR THE BORDER
BAD HOMBRE

*James Allenvale 'Bunduki' Gunn
series*
THE AMAZONS OF
  ZILLIKIAN★
BUNDUKI
BUNDUKI AND DAWN
SACRIFICE FOR THE
  QUAGGA GOD
FEARLESS MASTER OF
  THE JUNGLE

Miscellaneous titles
J. T'S HUNDREDTH
J. T'S LADIES
SLAUGHTER'S WAY
TWO MILES TO THE
  BORDER
SLIP GUN
BLONDE GENIUS (*written in
  collaboration with Peter
  Clawson*)

★*Awaiting publication*

YOUNG OLE DEVIL

CORGI BOOKS
A DIVISION OF TRANSWORLD PUBLISHERS LTD

For the two beautiful Barbaras (French
and Innes, in alphabetical order) of the
White Lion Hotel, Melton Mowbray,
although this probably won't induce them to
serve me an extra pint of lager-and-lime
after closing time.

YOUNG OLE DEVIL
A CORGI BOOK 0 552 09650 4

First publication in Great Britain 1975

PRINTING HISTORY
Corgi edition published 1975
Corgi edition reprinted 1981

Copyright © J. T. Edson 1975

This book is set in 10pt Plantin

Corgi Books are published by
Transworld Publishers Ltd.,
Century House, 61-63 Uxbridge Road,
Ealing, London, W5 5SA
Made and printed in Great Britain by
Hunt Barnard Printing Ltd., Aylesbury, Bucks.

YOUNG OLE DEVIL

author's note: *This to explain briefly how the events recorded in YOUNG OLE DEVIL were caused and came about.*

Early in February 1836 a Mexican army was marching northwards, its numbers increasing as the Militia of various States and other volunteer regiments were called into service by *Presidente* Antonio Lopez de Santa Anna. Having consolidated his position as absolute dictatorial ruler of all Mexico south of the *Rio Bravo*,* *el Presidente* was intending to crush the opposition to his control of Texas.

Neither the Spanish Constitution nor the various régimes which had supplanted it after the formation of the Republic of Mexico in 1822 had ever made a serious effort towards opening up, developing, or even utilizing to any great extent, the vast area of land which they had named 'Texas' after the Tejas Indians who had occupied a portion of it. Instead, it had fallen upon foreigners to do so.

Having received a land grant on the Brazos River in 1821, Stephen F. Austin had been encouraged to form a swiftly-growing Anglo-U.S. community. Other grants – such as that acquired by the Hardin, Fog and Blaze clan on the Rio Hodo – had been made by the Spanish and earlier Mexican régimes and had allowed the Texians† to extend their holdings. By 1830, there were close to 15,000 of them living in the hitherto unoccupied and unproductive territory.

Such immigrants had proved to be beneficial to their adopted country. Hard-working and industrious for the most part, they had been willing to improve and develop the land which they were occupying. Being capable fighting men, skilled in the use of weapons, they had been able to stand up against the hostile bands of Commanche, Wichita, Tonkawa and

*Rio Bravo: the Mexicans' name for the Rio Grande.

† Texian: an Anglo-U.S.-born citizen of Texas, the 'i' being dropped from usage after the Mexican War of 1846–48.

7

Kiowa Indians and, unlike many of the *Chicano** population, did not expect, or require the protection of the Mexican army against such foes. Furthermore, as they had increased the potential value of their properties, they had formed a useful source of revenue of the Mexican economy.

However, despite all of the financial and other benefits which had accrued from the Anglo-U.S. colonists, the authorities in Mexico City had grown less and less enamoured by the prospect of an ever-increasing foreign population, even when it was occupying and making productive land for which they had little use themselves. Diverse languages, customs and, in some cases, religious beliefs had combined with basic differences between the Texians' and the Mexicans' conceptions of democratic government to form constant sources of friction.

The incessant political upheavals, as one unstable régime after another gained power, caused a growing sense of discontent among the Texians. Each successive party to form a government had appeared to be worse than its predecessors. Fully occupied with trying to remain in office, none had given any consideration to the immigrants' request that Texas be established as a separate State – it was regarded as a territory of the State of Coahuila – with representation in the government. They had, nevertheless, continued to levy taxes and duties against the Texians and had attempted to deny entry to further immigrants. As the Texians who had already become established, and not a few of the *Chicanos* had pointed out, such a prohibition would ruin all hope of further expansion and revelopment.

While the majority of the Texians had accepted Mexican citizenship in good faith, the refusal to grant representation, and other treatment to which they had been subjected by the various régimes caused them to revise their atitudes. More and more of them had come to agree with the faction, amongst which Samuel Houston had been prominent, which had insisted that the only secure future for themselves and their descendants lay in the annexation of Texas by the United States of America.

On coming into power, Santa Anna had quickly shown signs of being more ruthless, vindictive and oppressive than any of his predecessors. Adopting the invariable tactics of every dictator or despotic régime who seeks to impose his, or its, will

* Chicano: a Mexican-born citizen of Texas.

8

upon a population, he had decreed that the ownership of firearms was illegal and had sent an order to his brother-in-law, General Martin Perfecto de Cós, that all the Texians were to be disarmed.

Santa Anna's edict regarding firearms proved to be the final straw which had broken the colonists' patience. The Texians had realized that to surrender their weapons would leave them defenceless against the hostile Indians and criminal elements, none of whom would have given up *their* arms. What was more, it would effectively prevent the immigrants from resisting further impositions by *el Presidente*.

When the garrisons of the Mexican army – showing an energy which had been noticeably absent when called upon to deal with Indians or *bandidos* – attempted to carry out the disarmament, the Texians had refused to obey. There had been rioting and open conflict at Anahuac, Gonzales, Velasco and other places. Such had been the fury of the Texians' resistance that most of the Mexican troops had been compelled to fall back and join General Cós at San Antonio de Bexar. Faced with what amounted to an open rebellion by men who still possessed the means to resist and were generally superior to his own soldiers in the handling of weapons, Cós had not been able to enforce *el Presidente's* wishes. Nor, despite having been aware of the gravity of the situation, had he attempted to have the disarmament edict rescinded or tried to bring about a peaceful settlement.

Realizing that there was no hope of obtaining an amicable and satisfactory relationship with Santa Anna, the Texians had decided to sever all connections with Mexico. They had set up a provisional government, with Henry Smith and James W. Robinson as Governor and Lieutenant Governor respectively and had sent a commission headed by Stephen F. Austin to the United States to try and obtain arms and provisions. Samuel Houston had been appointed major general and made responsible for organizing an army to defend what would – at least until annexation by the United States, which everybody was confident would be a foregone conclusion, be an independent republic under the Lone Star flag. Prominent and wealthy Texians, such as James Bowie, William Barrett Travis, Edward Burleson, Benjamin Milam, the Fog brothers, Edward and Marsden, James W. Fannin and Frank Johnson, had raised regiments – few of which had a strength exceeding two hundred men – so as to be ready to meet the attempts which all knew Santa Anna would make to subdue their bid for independence.

The earlier stages of the rebellion had been successful as far as the Texians were concerned. Several minor skirmishes had gone in their favour, as had the only major confrontation to have taken place. On December the 11th, 1835, after a battle which had lasted for six days, Cós and his force of eleven hundred men had surrendered to Colonels Milam and Burleson at San Antonio de Bexar. Although there had been objections from some of the other senior officers in the Republic of Texa's army, the co-commanders had allowed all of their captives to return unharmed to Mexico on Cós having given his parole that he and his men would not participate in further military action against the Texians. If the reports which had been brought in by the Texians' scouts had been correct, the protest of some officers had been justifiable. Cós was accompanying his brother-in-law and clearly did not intend to honour the conditions of his parole.

While the various successes had boosted the morale of the Republic of Texas's army, they had proved a mixed blessing in that they presented an incorrect impression of the struggle which still lay ahead. The victories, as Houston and most of his senior officers appreciated, had been achieved against poorly-trained, badly-equipped, and indifferently commanded troops.

Due to Texas being so far from the centre of their country's affairs and offering few opportunites for gaining distinction and promotion, career-conscious officers of good quality had avoided serving there. Houston knew that such men would now be coming and would command battle-tried battalions which had fought in the various struggles between the factions who were attempting to take over the reins of government. They would be a much more dangerous proposition than anything so far faced by the Texians. Not only that, the Mexicans would have a tremendous advantage in numbers.

Being aware of the disparity of the size of his own command and the army which Santa Anna would be able to put into the field, Houston had been disinclined to meet the Mexicans in open battle except upon his own terms and on ground of his choosing. With that in mind, he had ordered all the scattered regiments and people in the western sector to assemble at San

Antonio de Bexar. Once they had done so, it was his intention to withdraw into East Texas and make their stand where, if things should go against them, they would have an avenue of escape by crossing the border into the United States.

Although many of the Texians who would be compelled to abandon their homes had seen the wisdom of withdrawing, realizing that *el Presidente* would show them no mercy if he laid hands on them, not all had done so. Four hundred men, under the command of Colonel Fannin, had declared that they would not retreat and intended to hold the town of Goliad.

There was, however, another and more serious threat to the unity of what remained of Houston's army. Eager for fame, acclaim and glory, Colonel Frank Johnson was planning to invade Mexico along the Gulf Coast route and was willing to go to any lengths to make his scheme succeed.

CHAPTER ONE

I'M FIGHTING FOR THE LIKES OF *THEM!*

'I DON'T doubt Sam Houston's courage, or his integrity,'
Stanforth Duke stated, after one of the men who had accompanied him to San Antonio and was mingling with the
other customers, acting as a stranger, had asked for his views on
the current situation. Since entering the Little Sisters *Cantina*,
he had spent much money buying drinks and had made himself
so popular that he felt sure that the crowd would be willing to
listen to him. Knowing that there would be some present who
held the Commanding General of the Republic of Texas's
army in high esteem, he did not want to antagonize them by too
blatant a criticism of their hero. 'But I do question his judgement when he talks of burning homes and crops,* then running
away from the Mexicans. Don't get me wrong, though, I've no
stake in this personally. I live up north near Shelbyville. But if
my home was down in this part of the country, I'd be damned if
I'd be willing to put a torch to it, up stakes and run. Especially
as we've licked the greasers every time we've locked horns with
'em.'

'It ain't right for you to be talking that ways, stranger,' protested a second member of Duke's party, who was sitting at a
table some disance away from the first man. 'You know the
General figures that's the right thing to do.'

'With respect sir, I don't agree that I shouldn't be saying

---

* In addition to withdrawing, Houston had wanted to adopt what
would one day become known as a 'scorched earth' policy. He had
sound reasons for such a measure. By burning their homes, crops and
other foodstuffs which they could not carry with them, the Texians
would have left their enemies with a difficult supply problem which
would increase, rather than diminish, the further Santa Anna advanced
beyond the Rio Grande. Despite having this explained to them, there
had been such strenuous opposition and refusal that Houston had been
compelled to drop the proposal.

Sam Houston's wrong in how he wants to handle things,' Duke answered. The interruption had been made to anticipate any similar protest from genuine supporters of the General. 'The way I figure it, the Republic of Texas's a free country where a man's entitled to speak his mind about anything, or *anybody*, no matter how important they be. That's one of the reasons we've taken up arms against Santa Anna.'

Having delivered the comment, the burly, well-dressed man paused so as to study the response to it. Clearly nobody suspected that he and the lanky, buckskin-clad protestor were working together. There was a brief, yet general rumble of agreement. Satisfied that he had made his point and would be allowed to continue without interruption, he swept his gaze around the crowded bar-room.

The customers who had assembled at the Little Sisters *Cantina* shortly after noon on February the 18th, 1836, were a cross-section of the male Texian population who had gathered at San Antonio in answer to Houston's summons. Some of them had on home-spun garments of the style common among the poorer communities of the United States. There were others clad in buckskins, after the fashion of the mountain men. Several wore clothing derived from the working attire of the Mexican *vaqueros* which was in the process of evolving into the traditional dress of the Texas cowhands. A few, such as Duke, sported broadcloth or cheaper styles of town suits. Scattered among them were a number of soldiers whose fatigue uniforms – black leather, *kepi*-like forage caps which could be folded flat for packing; waist-length dark blue tunics that had high, stiff stand-up collars but lacked the pipe-clayed white crossbelts; lighter blue trousers decorated by stripes along the outer seams of the legs; black boots with spurs on the heels – had been copied, with minor variations, from the United States' Regiment of Dragoons by Colonel William Barrett Travis and supplied to the members of his command.

Although only Travis's men wore recognizable uniforms, Duke knew that there were representatives of every regiment in the vicinity present. So he had an audience which was ideally suited for his purposes. He had come to San Antonio with the dual purpose of recruiting men for the force with which Colonel Frank Johnson was planning to invade Mexico, and to persuade those who remained to compel Houston to make a stand instead of withdrawing. If the latter could be achieved,

14

the attention of the whole of the Mexican army would be directed against Houston and it would greatly increase Johnson's chances of success. Neither Johnson nor Duke were over concerned with the adverse effect such a stand might, probably would, have upon the General's outnumbered force.

'What'd you-all reckon we should do, mister?' asked a stocky man in a cheap town suit, from another part of the room.

'Attack the greasers before they can even cross the Rio Grande,' Duke replied, accepting the cue which had been fed by the third of his associates. 'That way, there'll be no call for you to leave the homes you've worked so hard to build. You'll stop the greasers before they can get near to them.'

'By cracky, that's right!' enthused the stocky man and there was another mutter of fairly general approval.

Standing behind the bar, William Cord listened to the conversation with considerable misgivings as he guessed what it was leading up to. It was probably the last opportunity that Cord would have to do business for some time and he had benefited by the amount of money which Duke had spent. For all that, he wished the burly man had stayed away from his *cantina*. Being whole-heartedly in favour of Houston's strategy, even though following it would mean that he must abandon his hitherto lucrative place of business, he did not approve of what he guessed was a carefully organized attempt to change it.

However, after the clever way in which Duke had established his right to freedom of expression, Cord could not see any way of preventing him from airing his views. For the *cantina's* owner – a known supporter of Houston's policies – to attempt any kind of intervention would, he realized, evoke protests which might erupt into open conflict between those who were in favour of the General's strategy and those who opposed it. Cord suspected that the men who had supplied the various comments were in cahoots with Duke. He had a good idea that there were at least two more of the agitator's companions in the room, although as yet they had not spoken. Big, burly, unshaven, dressed in poor quality town suits with grubby, collarless white shirts, they had a strong family resemblance which suggested they might be brothers. Like the other customers who were lining the bar almost elbow to elbow, they were standing with their backs to Cord. However, instead of looking at Duke, they were watching the crowd.

Turning his gaze in the pair's direction, Cord noticed a man coming through the batwing doors. Approaching the counter, the newcomer moved with a Gascon swagger which reminded the owner of the arrogant, over-proud, French-Creole dandies he had seen in New Orleans. Although he was not French, the man exuded a similar cocky self-importance and – assurance. His clothing was clean and he had a well-scrubbed look.

Bare-headed, with his wide-brimmed, low-crowned black hat dangling by its fancy *barbiquejo* chin-strap on to his back, the young man – he would be in his mid-twenties – was six foot in height and had a straight-backed, whipcord lean frame which was set off to its best advantage by his well-tailored garments. He had a thinly-rolled silk bandana which was a glorious riot of brilliant, if clashing, colours knotted about his throat so that its long ends trailed over the breast of his open-necked fringed buckskin shirt. His tight-fitting fawn riding breeches ended in the tops of highly-polished Hessian boots. The belt into which he had hooked his thumbs carried a long-bladed, clip-pointed knife – of the type made by James Black, the Arkansas master-cutler, which had already become known as a 'bowie', in honour of the man who had designed the original – in a decorative Indian sheath at the left side. There was a slanting, two inch broad leather loop attached to the right side of the belt. Into this was thrust the barrel of a good quality pistol so that the butt was pointing forward and would be available to the grasp of either hand.

However, it was the newcomer's face which attracted Cord's main attention. The black hair was taken back in a way which made the sides above his temples protrude and look like short horns. That combined with the brows of his coal black eyes that were shaped like inverted 'V's', an aquiline nose, a neatly trimmed moustache and short chin beard gave his features an almost Satanic expression.

Coming to a halt on spread-apart feet, the newcomer studied the crowded front of the bar. Then his eyes came to rest upon the two men whom Cord suspected of being members of the agitator's party. Becoming aware of the scrutiny, the pair turned their eyes towards the man who was looking at them.

'Would you *gentlemen* mind moving so that *I* can get through to the bar?' the young dandy inquired, his voice that of a well-educated Southron.

Seeing the pair stiffen as if somebody had laid a quirt across their rumps, Cord could tell that they did not care for the manner in which they were being addressed. Politely worded though the appeal had been, the speaker's tone and attitude were more suitable to the deliverance of a demand which he believed he had every right to make. Everything about him suggested that he felt he was dealing with unimportant social inferiors.

A shrewd judge of character, Cord concluded that the newcomer's behaviour was more liable to rouse the two men's wrath than to lead them into compliance with his wishes.

'Come on now!' the young dandy continued impatiently, raising his voice and causing it to sound even more autocratically commanding. 'Step out of the way there and let me through!'

Such was not, Cord could have warned the newcomer, the wisest way in which to speak to two obvious bullies and roughnecks. They were certain to take exception to his assumption of superiority and would be most unlikely to treat him with the servile deference that he clearly considered he should receive.

'Can't rightly see no reason why we should,' the slightly taller and older of the pair stated, conscious of the glances being darted at them by their immediate neighbours along the bar. 'Can you, Brother Basil?'

'I ain't got no better eye-sight 'n you-all, Brother Cyril,' the second man answered, scowling balefully at the dandy. 'Which being so, I'd say you should try it on some other place, fancy pants. We ain't a-fixing to move.'

The brothers had loud, harsh voices which they made no attempt to modulate. So their words were spreading beyond the person at whom they were being directed. Several pairs of eyes swung away from Duke as he was starting to explain how Johnson's proposed invasion of Mexico would benefit the Republic of Texas.

'Now look here, you two!' the dandy said coldly, also raising his voice to a level which was louder than necessary. 'While the likes of you have been propping up a bar, I've been out scouting against the Mexicans. So move aside and let me through.'

Glancing around as he heard the voices and noticed that he was losing the attention of his audience, Duke located the cause of the disturbance. The discovery caused him mingled annoyance and anxiety. He had spent a fair sum of money, buying drinks to ingratiate himself with the crowd and make them

2   17

more receptive to his agitation, so he did not want anything to distract them. From what he could see and hear, there might be a serious distraction developing. Of all the men in the room, the arrogant young dandy could hardly have selected two more dangerous than the Winglow brothers upon whom to try and impose his imperious wishes.

Being aware of the delicate nature of his assignment, Duke had tried to impress upon all his escort the need to avoid trouble if possible. He had repeated his reminder at Shelby's Livery Barn where they had left their horses before coming separately to the *cantina*. Clearly Cyril Winglow, who was always a bad-tempered bully, had forgotten his instructions.

'He's sure dressed fancy for a feller's done all that there scouting, ain't he Brother Basil?' Cyril asked, looking the young man over from head to foot.

'Don't let the way I look fool you, *hombre*,' the dandy advised, his Mephistophelian features growing even more sardonic and mocking as he returned the scrutiny. 'I've done plenty of fighting in this war. So I don't need to go around hawg-filthy to try to make folks think I have.'

'Hey there, gentlemen!' Duke called, seeing the anger which came to the brothers' faces as the barb went home. Hearing him, they looked in his direction and he hoped that they would take a hint from his intervention. 'Let's have no unpleasantness.'

'There won't be any,' the young dandy replied, but destroyed the relief which Duke had started to feel by continuing, 'Just so long as these two yahoos stop hogging the bar and let me through.'

'Here, sir,' Duke put in hurriedly, speaking before either of the brothers could do more than stare at the newcomer. Oozing an amiable bonhomie which he was far from feeling, he stepped forward and waved a hand to the gap he had left at the counter. 'You can have my place.'

'Thank you for the offer, sir,' the dandy drawled, without moving or taking his attention from the brothers. 'But I want *them* to make way for me. Damn it, I'm fighting for the likes of them!'

'Fighting for—!' Cyril began, slamming his glass down so that it shattered on the floor.

'Hold it!' Cord bellowed, snatching up and cocking the bell-mouthed blunderbuss which he kept on a shelf under the counter. 'She's loaded with rock-salt and I'll use her should I have to.'

'Are you siding with him?' Cyril demanded, spitting the words over his shoulder. However, having heard the menacing clicking as the weapon's hammer was drawn back, he stood still instead of leaping at the newcomer.

'I'm not siding with anybody,' Cord corrected. 'Just protecting my property is all. If you feller's got things to settle, go outside and do it.'

Although Cord had acted instinctively in the first place, his training as the owner of a *cantina* having taught him the advisability of trying to prevent trouble on his premises, he had seen how he might turn the present situation to good use. If the men went outside to fight, the majority – if not all – of the other customers would follow to watch. That would put a temporary stop to the agitator's speech-making and allow Cord to send his son with a warning of what was happening to General Houston's headquarters.

'Surely there's no need for that, gentlemen,' Duke protested in a placatory manner, duplicating Cord's thoughts on how the crowd would react. He moved closer, looking at the brothers rather than their challenger. 'At a time like this, we can't have fighting amongst ourselves.'

'I shouldn't reckon they'd want to do any fighting with anybody,' the dandy scoffed.

'Easy, Brother Cyril!' Basil said urgently, having taken notice of their leaders's obvious disapproval. While just as much a bully as his sibling, he was somewhat more intelligent. Being aware of how vindictive Duke could behave when crossed, Basil had no wish to antagonize him. There was, he decided, a way out which would avoid any suggestion of them having backed down. 'He's got a knife 'n' pistol and neither of us is armed.'

Realizing what the younger Winglow had in mind, Duke nodded approvingly. Nobody could blame the brothers for refusing to take on an armed man when neither was carrying weapons. Nor was it likely that the arrogant young dandy would be willing to consider fighting with this bare hands against a heavier opponent.

It was a good try, but failed to produce the desired result.

'Shucks, I'd hate the gents here to think I'd need weapons to deal with the likes of you,' the young man remarked, sliding the knife from its sheath with his left hand while the right pulled the pistol clear of the loop. 'If somebody will hold these for me—'

'Here, mister,' offered the burly sergeant of Travis's regiment, who was sitting at a table near to the dandy. He came to his feet and held out his hands, 'I'll take them for you.'

'*Gracias*,' the young man drawled, relinquishing the weapons without hesitation. Then he swung his sardonic gaze to Cyril and went on. 'Now it's entirely up to you, loud mouth. *I'm* ready, but *you* might not have the stomach for it.'

'I'll show you whether I have, or—!' Cyril roared furiously, ignoring Duke's prohibitive head-shake and making as if to lunge at his tormentor.

'Not in here, you won't!' Cord interrupted firmly, tapping the muzzle of his blunderbuss on the counter to give emphasis to his words. 'If you're set on fighting, go outside where my furniture won't get broken.'

'That suits me fine,' the young man announced as, taking heed of the owner's words and action, Cyril restrained his impulse to attack. 'I'll be waiting out there, loud mouth. You do what you want.'

With that, the dandy swung on his heel and swaggered towards the door. He presented his back contemptuously to the brothers and did not so much as glance over his shoulder as he left the building.

'Damn it to hell, Major Duke!' Cyril protested, turning to the agitator and, in his desire to exculpate himself, ignoring the fact that they were not supposed to know each other. 'The son-of-a-bitch ain't giving me no choice.'

An almost uncontrollable rage filled Duke as he watched Cyril removing his hat and coat, but the incautious words had not caused it. Probably nobody else had attached any significance to them. All around the room, men were finishing their drinks and shoving back their chairs. Duke's anger was rising as he saw that what he had feared was happening.

'Hey!' whooped a soldier excitedly, as Cyril passed the garments to Basil and set off across the room. 'Come on. Let's go see what happens.'

Watching the mass movement to go outside, Duke knew that he could neither do nor say anything to prevent the disruption of his work. Stimulated by the drinks which he had bought for them, the crowd clearly considered that watching a fight would be more interesting and entertaining than listening to him. Duke silently cursed the brothers for not having remembered why they were in San Antonio and refusing to make room for the newcomer at the bar. One glance at him ought to have warned them that their response would make such a proud, arrogant young hot-head determined to enforce his demand.

'By cracky, mister,' enthused a leathery, buckskin-clad old timer who was standing at Duke's side, breaking in on his train of thought. 'That feller's going to get taught a lesson. It don't pay to rile up young Cap'n Hardin that ways.'

'Who?' the agitator inquired, realizing that the other did not consider the 'lesson' would be given by Cyril Winglow.

'Cap'n Jackson Baines Hardin of the Texas Light Cavalry,' the leathery man elaborated. 'He's a lil ole devil in a fight.'

CHAPTER TWO

LET'S SEE HOW YOU STACK UP
AGAINST A *MAN*

STANDING in the centre of the street, Jackson Baines Hardin watched the crowd streaming out of the Little Sisters *Cantina*. They spread each way along the sidewalk, talking excitedly, making bets and jostling each other for the best positions from which to see what happened. If he was perturbed by what he had done inside, his Mephistophelian features – which, in part, accounted for his generally, used nickname 'Ole Devil'* – showed no evidence of it. Rather, if his expression was anything to go by, he regarded the prospect of fighting with a heavier man as an enjoyable relaxation from the serious and dangerous business of scouting against the Mexican army.

There was a hush as the Winglow brothers emerged, with Basil carrying Cyril's hat and jacket. While the young man's comments had been directed at both of them, they had realized that the crowd would not allow them to make a combined attack upon him. Nor, if it came to a point, did either believe that it would be necessary to do so. Each of them was heavier than the slim dandy and they had both acquired considerable ability at rough-house brawling.

'Sorry you ain't going to get a chance to whip him, Brother Basil,' Cyril announced as he lumbered from the sidewalk.

'That's all right,' Basil answered, halting at the edge alongside the sergeant who had taken charge of Hardin's property. 'You go do it good, Brother Cyril.'

Even as the younger brother gave his magnanimous blessing, Hardin showed a reluctance to wait for Cyril to come to him. Instead, he darted forward. Doubting that the young man intended to meet him toe-to-toe, Cyril lunged forward and

* Another reason for the nickname had arisen out of the fact that other men before the old timer in the *cantina* had commented upon him being a 'lil ole devil' in a fight.

22

spread open his arms. By doing so, he intended to circumvent the other's attempt to swerve by at the last moment. He discovered too late that such had never been Hardin's plan.

Gauging the distance which was separating them, Hardin bounded into the air as he had been taught by a master of *savate* – the French style of foot and fist fighting – in New Orleans. Drawing up his knees towards his chest, he caused his body to tilt backwards. Then, straightening his legs, he propelled the soles of his Hessian boots into the centre of Cyril's chest. All the air was driven from the burly man's lungs and he was flung backwards by the powerful, unexpected attack. To the accompaniment of laughter and startled comments from the onlookers, he collided with the left side hitching rail. That alone prevented him from falling on to the sidewalk.

Rebounding from the leaping high kick, Hardin landed on his feet with an almost cat-like agility. He clearly had every intention of following up his advantage before his opponent could recover. Gliding forward, he smashed his left fist into Cyril's belly. As the man gasped and started to fold at the waist, Hardin's clenched right hand rose to meet the bristle-covered chin. Lifted erect and held that way by the stout bar of the hitching-rail, dazed and winded, Cyril was in serious trouble. He was clearly unable to stop the continuation of the attack.

Seeing his brother's predicament, Basil set about relieving it. Dropping Cyril's coat and hat, he sprang forward without waiting to remove his own. Before Hardin realized that Basil had intervened, he felt a hand grasping the back of his shirt collar and another catching his right wrist to twist it into a hammerlock.

Having obtained his two holds, Basil tried to use them as a means of pushing the young dandy away from his brother. Allowing himself to go until he had regained his equilibrium, Hardin came to a stop when sure of it. Setting his weight on his left leg, he thrust his right diagonally until it was alongside Basil's left foot. Doing so caused his body to swing to the right and he crouched slightly, bending his left arm at the elbow. Although he had not tried to jerk his right wrist from Basil's right hand, the turning motion had brought it from behind his back. Giving the other no chance to return it to the hammerlock, he snapped it upwards with his palm towards his attacker. Doing so caused Basil to loosen his hold a little.

23

Instantly, Hardin's left knuckles ploughed into Basil's *solar plexus*. Letting out a croak, Basil released hardin's shirt and felt the wrist snatched away from his fingers. Coming around, Hardin delivered a right cross to Basil's jaw which turned him in a half circle. Nor did he let it end there. Bringing up his left boot, he rammed it hard against the seat of the younger brother's trousers and pushed hard. Unable to help himself, Basil went staggering to fall on hands and knees half way across the street.

Brief though the respite had been, Cyril had recovered sufficient of his wits to take action. Shoving away from the hitching rail, he swung a wide, looping round-house punch which struck the side of the young man's face. Although the attack came just too late to save Basil and, due to Cyril still being somewhat dazed, arrived with less than his full strength behind it, the blow caught Hardin before his foot had returned to the ground. Pitched sideways, he knew that he could not prevent himself from falling. So he let himself go and concentrated on landing as gently as possible. Alighting on the street, he rolled on to his back.

Lumbering forward, while his brother was rising, Cyril dropped with big hand driving forward to clamp on to Hardin's throat. It was also his intention to ram his right knee into the dandy's body. Although Hardin could not escape the hands, he managed to writhe so that the knees missed. That made his position a little easier, but he knew that he was far from being out of the woods. Kneeling at his side, Cyril raised his head with the intention of banging it on the ground. At the same time, Basil was running forward to help with the attack.

Strolling from an alley along the street, a man of about Hardin's age stopped as he saw what was happening. Six foot tall, heavily built, he conveyed an impression of well-padded, comfortable lethargy. He had curly, auburn hair showing beneath his black hat, and his sun-reddened fetures lost their amiable, sleepy-looking expression as he took in the scene before the *cantina*. As he was dressed – with the exception of his scarlet silk bandana – and armed in the same fashion as Hardin, it seemed likely that he was connected in some way with the dandy. He too appeared to have bathed, shaved and donned clean garments recently, Although his pace changed from a leisurely amble to a run, he knew that he would not be able to reach the fight before the second assailant had returned to participate in it.

Being unaware that help was coming, Hardin set about saving himself. Bracing his neck, without making what he knew would be a futile attempt to free it by sheer strength, he managed to lessen the impact as Cyril shoved downwards and the back of his head met the ground. Then, as he was raised for a second time, he pivoted at the hips to send his left knee with some force into the burly man's ribs. Immediately after making that attack, Hardin thrust his right hand upwards between Cyril's arms. He did not close it into a fist. Instead, he jabbed his first and second fingers into Cyril's nostrils. Pain roared through the recipient of the attack. Leaving Hardin's throat, his hands went up to try and staunch the blood which gushed from his nose.

Rushing up, Basil arrived just after his brother had been compelled to release Hardin. Coming in from the opposite side to Cyril, Basil launched his right foot in a kick. Rolling to the left, Hardin swung his left arm so that the base of his fist met the advancing shin just above the ankle. Working in smooth co-ordination, his right hand grasped the leg of the trousers over his left fist. Having halted the kick, Hardin returned his shoulders to the ground and hauled the captured limb above him. Then his own right leg snapped around and upwards, aiming the toe of his boot at Basil's groin area. The kick caught Basil on the inside of the upper thigh. While painful, it was not sufficiently so to incapacitate him. It did, however, combine with the pull being exerted upon his leg to throw him off balance.

Giving Basil's leg a twisting heave which toppled him over, Hardin released him and bounded up. Snarling incoherently in his rage, half-blinded by tears, Cyril lunged and with bloody hands tried to grab the slim young man.

'This's for the *Chicano* boy!' Hardin told the burly man savagely, pivoting into another *savate* kick.

Propelled by the powerful gluteus muscles of Hardin's buttocks, his right boot came into contact with the bottom of Cyril's jaw. The burly man's head hinged back until it seemed that his neck might be in danger of snapping. Lifted from his knees he began to crumple like a punctured balloon and collapsed flaccidly on to his face.

Having disposed of the elder brother, Hardin turned his attention to the younger. Moving clear of Cyril and standing with his back to the spectators, the young dandy studied Basil who was once more on his hands and knees and staring at his sibling as if unable to believe his eyes.

'Come on, you lousy son-of-a-bitch!' Hardin ordered coldly and his face seemed even more Satanic as he swept the second of the Winglow family with a contempt-filled gaze. 'Let's see how you stack up against a *man* instead of a *Chicano* boy.'

Swinging his head so as to glare at the speaker, Basil became aware of the significance of the comment and did not care for what it suggested. Apparently the dandy had another reason besides arrogant self-importance for picking the fight.

Although the Winglows and their companions had believed that they were the only human occupants of the livery barn, they had been mistaken. Shortly after the rest of the party had taken their departure, the brothers had heard a scuffling noise. On going to investigate, they had discovered that a pair of boys – a Texian and a *Chicano* – were hiding behind some bales of hay. Guessing that the boys had heard Duke giving his instructions, Basil and Cyril had decided to frighten them into keeping quiet and had tried to catch them. Being older than his friend, the *Chicano* had tried to hold the brothers off with a pitchfork while the youngster escaped. Although he had been partly successful, the Texian boy having fled, the *Chicano* had been less fortunate. Disarming him, the brothers had slapped him around and finally left him bloody and unconscious on the floor.

Partly because they had been told to pretend that they did not know the rest of their party, but mainly due to believing that Duke would disapprove of what they had done, the brothers had not mentioned the incident on their arrival at the *cantina*. From what he had said, it seemed that the dandy had found the *Chicano* and, learning who was responsible, had for some reason decided to inflict summary punishment upon the men who had carried out the attack.

Letting out a bellow of rage, Basil thrust himself erect. Recklessly he flung himself forward with big hands reaching to grab hold of the dandy. It proved to be a costly error in tactics. Before his fingers could close, the object of his intentions seemed to disappear.

Crouching under Basil's grasp, Hardin let him have a punch

in the pit of the stomach. It halted him and, as he doubled over, Hardin's knee rocketed upwards. For the second time, Basil was fortunate in avoiding the full force of an attack. He had fallen back just enough for the knee to miss his face. Struck on the forehead, he was lifted upright and staggered rearwards for a few steps. However, he did not go down. As Hardin advanced, Basil caught his balance and swung a backhand blow with his right hand. Although it was almost at the end of its flight when it connected on the side of the dandy's head, it brought him to a halt. Basil followed it with a much more effective punch to the chest, sending Hardin up against the hitching rail. Wanting to make the most of his success, Basil lunged forward.

On seeing that his cousin had escaped and rendered one attacker *hors-de-combat*, Mannen Blaze had slowed to a more leisurely pace. He had complete faith in Hardin's ability to take care of the remaining assailant. Satisfied that his assistance would not be required and thinking that his arrival might bring some of the burly man's friends into the affair, he halted and leaned against the hitching rail of a store on the opposite side of the street to the *cantina*. While it was clear that he did not mean to intervene, he was ready if anybody else should do so. Although he did not know it, such an intervention was at that moment being suggested.

Standing glowering angrily at the crowd, Duke felt a touch on his sleeve. Looking around he found one of his party at his side. Tall, gangling, the man's sombre features and black clothing were indicative of his profession. He had been an undertaker before joining Johnson's regiment.

'Shall we cut in, major?' the man inquired, watching Hardin side-step Basil's rush and move into the centre of the street.

'No, Jolly!' Duke replied. 'Those two stupid bastards deserve all they get, letting themselves be riled into a fight.'

The force with which the punch had landed on his chest had been a warning to Hardin that a toe-to-toe slugging brawl would favour his heavier assailant. So he had had no intention of being trapped in a position which would require that he fought in such a manner. Having evaded Basil and gained room to manoeuvre, he swung around to await the next development.

Instead of having learned the futility of such tactics, the burly man continued with the methods he had employed with

27

some success in previous fights. They proved disastrous against the swiftly-moving dandy, who refused to stand and trade blows or to come to grips where brute strength would have prevailed. It soon became obvious that, barring something unforeseen happening, Hardin was going to win. However, not all of the punishment being meted out went one way, Basil managed to land some punches in return for the many which were being rained upon him. All in all, the appreciative spectators were treated to a pretty good fight.

Despite seeing that his cousin was justifying his confidence, Mannen Blaze was perturbed as he remembered what had brought them to San Antonio. Devil could, Blaze reflected have picked a more suitable time to become involved in a street brawl. That belief was increased, as was his perturbation, by the sight of two men who came from an alley further along the street. Recognizing one and making an accurate guess at the other's identity, Blaze could foresee stormy times ahead for his cousin.

One of the new arrivals was grey-haired, very tall, broad-shouldered and powerfully built. Clad in a buckskin shirt, brown bell-bottomed *vaquero* trousers and high heeled, spur-decorated boots, with a wide-brimmed black hat tilted back on his head, he had a bowie knife – more correctly *the* bowie knife* – in a sheath on the left side of his waist belt.

Seeing Colonel James Bowie approaching was not the cause of Blaze's consternation. In fact, the legendary knife-fighter and adventurer appeared to be amused at finding Hardin in a fight. The same did not apply to his companion.

Lacking two inches of Bowie's height, the second man was also more slenderly built. He wore a uniform similar to those of the soldiers on the sidewalk, except that it was of better material and more decorative. There were bullion shoulder scales on his tunic and his head-dress was a black felt *shako*. Further indications of his rank were supplied by the red sash, knotted at the right, around his waist under a belt with a sabre hanging by its slings, and by a row of five brass buttons on each sleeve's cuff. He marched rather than walked, striding out as if on parade.

Blaze assumed, correctly, that the officer was Colonel William Barrett Travis; already noted for being a tough martinet

* What happened to the knife after the Alamo is told in: *The Quest for Bowie's Blade.*

28

and disciplinarian. Judging from his expression, he did not approve of what was going on.

'Stop this damned brawling immediately!' Travis bellowed, just after Hardin had knocked Basil staggering with a right to the jaw.

Turning his head to discover who had spoken, Hardin duplicated his cousin's identification of the two men. However, carrying out the order was not possible. While Hardin was willing to obey, the same did not apply to his battered and bloody assailant.

Catching his balance and coming to a halt, Basil once again charged wildly at the young man who had inflicted so much pain upon him. Hearing the other approaching, Hardin knew that he would not be responsible to words. Avoiding the bull-like rush, he whipped around a *savate* circular side kick which propelled the toe of his boot into the pit of Basil's stomach with considerable force. The burly man let out a belching gasp, folded over at the waist and blundered onwards a couple of steps. Pivoting, Hardin delivered a second kick. It landed on the seat of Basil's pants and kept him moving. Pure chance guided him to the supporting post of the hitching rail. As he still had not straightened up, the top of his skull rammed into the sturdy timber. Rebounding from it, he fell as if he had been boned and with blood pouring from his scalp.

'Sorry, colonel,' Hardin said, breathing heavily but turning in a respectful manner towards the approaching men. 'I don't think that feller heard what you said.'

'I see you've not forgotten how to fight, young Ole Devil,' Bowie remarked with a grin, glancing at the motionless brothers.

'You know him, Colonel Bowie?' Travis asked, before Hardin could reply and in tones which suggested that he and the great knife fighter might not be on the best of terms.

'Don't you?' Bowie inquired, sounding puzzled. 'This's Captain Hardin of Ed Fog's Texas Light Cavalry. Devil, may I present Colonel William Barrett Travis?'

'My pleasure, sir,' Hardin responded, although he felt certain that the sentiment would not be mutual under the circumstances.

Like his cousin, who was coming slowly towards him, Hardin silently decided that of all the senior officers in the Republic of Texas's army, Barrett Travis was the last whom he would have wanted to arrive at that moment. Even if the colonel had known the reason for the fight, Hardin considered it was unlikely to have met with his approval.

'Sergeant Brill!' Travis called, turning to the spectators on the sidewalk, without offering to acknowledge the introduction. 'Take our men back to the camp and find them some work.'

'Yo!' answered the non-com, giving what was already developing into the accepted cavalry response to an order.

While Duke could see that he would be losing some of his audience, he expected that the rest were going to re-enter the *cantina* and allow him to continue with the work which had been interrupted. Even as the thought came, he heard bugles playing a familiar and – under the circumstances – infuriating call.

'That's assembly, boys,' Bowie announced. 'Means we're all wanted back at the camp. I'd be right obliged if you'd close down for a spell, Bill.'

'She's as good's done, Jim,' Cord answered, and he could hardly restrain his relief as he realized that by doing so he would prevent Duke from resuming the agitation. 'I'll open up after sundown, gents, but there'll be nothing else served until then. Collect your belongings.'

'Whose outfit are those two with?' Bowie asked, indicating the unconscious brothers.

Nobody replied. Glancing at Duke, his men received a prohibitive shake of his head and kept silent.

'Looks like they must have come in to join somebody,' Bowie went on. 'Here, Ed, Tim, see to them.'

The men named by the knife-fighter belonged to his regiment. Swinging from the porch, they went to carry out the order. While Travis's soldiers were forming up, the sergeant returned Hardin's property to him.

'We'd best have 'em toted to a doctor, Colonel Jim,' suggested one of the men who was examining the brothers, and he pointed to Basil. 'This jasper's head's split open pretty bad and, way young Ole Devil there kicked it, the other'll be lucky if his jaw's not broken.'

'That's *very* good!' Travis snorted, in tones which implied exactly the opposite, scowling at Hardin who had donned his hat and was returning the pistol to its loop on his belt. 'Thanks to you, *captain*, we've lost two men who could have fought against the Mexicans.'

30

'No excuse, sir,' the young dandy answered, stiffening into a ramrod straight brace as rigidly military as the uniformed colonel's posture. His Mephistophelian features displayed a complete lack of emotion, certainly he did not appear to be contrite over having deprived the army of the brothers' services. 'Permission to leave, sir?'

'Granted!' Travis replied. 'And, unless you wish to indulge in further brawls and to cripple a few more members of *our* army, I'd suggest that you get about whatever business has brought you to San Antonio.'

CHAPTER THREE

YOU'VE NO INTENTION OF BELIEVING US

'TOMMY'S not here yet,' Mannen Blaze remarked, looking languidly around as he and his cousin entered Shelby's Livery Barn.

'I was hoping that he wouldn't be,' Ole Devil Hardin admitted, and touched his bruised left cheek with a careful forefinger. 'With any luck, I'll have time to tidy myself up again before he comes to fetch us.'

'I'm going to stick with you this time, cousin,' Blaze declared with a sleepy grin. 'That way you'll maybe keep out of mischief.'

On their arrival at General Samuel Houston's headquarters that morning, Hardin and Blaze had delivered the report of the scouting mission which they had carried out. They had been told that the General would not be able to see them for some time, but wished to do so eventually. Wanting to look their best, and having an aversion to being dirty for longer than was necessary, they had left the third member of their party at the headquarters' building and gone to try and make themselves more presentable.

Visiting the livery barn where they had already left their horses, the cousins had asked advice of its owner. An old friend of their clan, Allen Shelby, had told them to go to his home and make use of his toilet facilities. As the senior officer, Hardin had been the first to use the bath and change from his travel-stained garments. While his cousin was bathing in turn, he had returned to the barn to see if their companion had arrived. Finding the *Chicano* boy and learning what had happened, he had set off to deal with the matter alone instead of waiting for Blaze to join him.

Although Hardin had achieved his purpose, he had accepted Colonel William Barrett Travis's comments and curt dismissal from the front of the *cantina* without making any attempt to offer an explanation which would exculpate him. Accompanied by his cousin, who had prudently remained in the background during the brief discussion with Travis, he had made his way back to the livery barn. They had arranged to meet their companion there when he came to fetch them for the interview with Houston.

During the walk from the *cantina* to the barn, Hardin had satisfied Blaze's curiosity regarding the trouble. He had also explained why he had not told Travis of the real reason for him picking the fight. Far from being the slow-witted dullard which he pretended to be, Blaze had conceded that his cousin had acted for the best and hoped that their superiors would share his sentiments when they heard.

The barn was still unoccupied, which did not surprise Hardin and Blaze. Shelby had been on the point of departing for a conference at Houston's headquarters when they had come to seek his advice, and had said that all of his employees were occupied with preparations for leaving with the army.

'Mrs. Shelby's too busy to want me bothering her again,' Hardin drawled. 'I'll have a wash in the horse-trough.'

'You shouldn't need to change your clothes again,' Blaze commented. 'I reckon we can brush most of the drift off.'

'I hope so,' Hardin replied. 'I don't have another pair of breeches until Mrs. Shelby sends the pair she's having washed. Let me get a towel out of my warbag and, while I'm washing, will you get the rest of our gear out of the office? Then we'll take the horses, go out to headquarters and wait there until the General can see us.'

'I'm for *that*,' Blaze declared. 'There'll be less chance of *you* getting into trouble again if we do.'

Although the cousins' and their companion's saddles were hanging with several more on the inverted V-shaped wooden 'burro', which had been erected along one wall for that purpose, they had removed their bed rolls, rifles and other weapons. Shelby had suggested that with so many strangers in town – and as the barn would be untended – it might be advisable for them to leave their more portable property somewhere less public than on the burro. Putting his private office at their disposal, he had given them a key so that they could retrieve their gear when they needed it.

By the time Hardin had finished his ablutions, Blaze had fetched their belongings from the office and had removed most

3

of the dirt stains from his shirt. Donning it, Hardin replaced the towel in his warbag. He was about to refold his bed roll when footsteps sounded and a group of men came through the open main doors.

Six in number, the newcomers formed a rough half circle and halted just inside the building. In the centre of the line, standing with his hands behind his back, was a tall, gangling, mournful-looking man wearing a black hat and suit. Studying him, Blaze thought he might be an undertaker and wondered what had brought him to the barn. Although the others wore a variety of clothing, it was clear that they were with the black dressed man. What was more, their attitude suggested that they might not have arrived for the harmless purpose of collecting their horses.

'What're you pair doing in here?' Erasmus Jolly demanded, after looking around to make sure that nobody else was present.

Having seen that he would not be able to carry out his assignment as long as the *cantina* was closed and the men returned to their regiments, Stanforth Duke had been furious. He had guessed that when Houston heard what he had been trying to do, he would take steps to ensure Duke was not given a second opportunity. Being of a vindictive nature he had decided that the indirect cause of his misfortune should be made to suffer. So he told Jolly to take their men and revenge themselves upon the young dandy, while he went to see if there was any chance of resuming the task which had brought them to San Antonio. Having discovered that their victim was at the livery barn, Jolly had come with his companions. He wanted to provoke Hardin into starting a fight so that he could claim, if questioned, that he and his companions had acted in self-defence. After what he had seen at the *cantina*, he felt confident that doing so would be easy.

'That depends on why you're asking,' Hardin answered truculently, coming to his feet and darting a quick look to where his pistol – which he had removed while washing – lay on his saddle just beyond his reach.

'There's a fair few fellers' gear in here, including our'n, with nobody to keep an eye on it,' growled the biggest of the party, standing to Jolly's right. Clad in *vanquero*-style clothing, his name was Stone. It had been he who had asked the questions in the *cantina* which had allowed Duke to start commenting upon

34

the military situation in Texas. 'So we're a mite curious when we find two fellers taking things out of somebody's warbag.'

'It's *my* warbag,' Hardin stated coldly, acting as Jolly hoped he would, and flickering a glance past the men towards the main entrance. 'And I'm putting something in, not taking it out.'

'How about them other two bed-rolls?' the former undertaker challenged, as he and his companions moved slowly closer. He still kept his hands behind his back and continued in an officious manner to which he felt sure the dandy would take exception, 'Seems to me that makes one more of 'em than there is of you.'

'We're taking our *amigo's* gear out to headquarters with us,' Blaze explained in a placatory manner, after having darted a look at his cousin which, Jolly believed, was imploring him not to make trouble.

'Your *amigo's*, huh?' Jolly sniffed and brought his party to a halt about fifteen feet away from the cousins.

'He's waiting out there,' Hardin elaborated and swung his gaze past the men as if searching for somebody to confirm his statement. Then he eyed the black dressed figure sardonically. 'Only you've no intention of believing us.'

'You're damned right we haven't,' Jolly confirmed, bringing his hands into view. The right was grasping a cocked pistol, which he lined at the slim young dandy. 'Stand still, both of you.'

'Best do it, Devil,' Blaze advised almost tremulously.

'Shed your weapons,' Jolly went on. 'We're going to take you to the constable and see what he reckons to your story.'

'That suits me,' Blaze declared, starting to draw the bowie knife from its sheath with the tips of his fingers. He looked at his cousin, continuing, 'I'd do it, was I you, Devil. The constable knows us and he'll soon clear things up.'

'That's for sure,' Hardin agreed, giving a confirmatory nod. Then he also took out his knife and let it fall. Oozing arrogance and indignation, he scowled at Jolly. 'And when he has, *hombre*, we'll be expecting an apology.'

'You'll get it,' the former undertaker sneered, watching the bulky red-head's pistol following the two knives. 'Move away from 'em.'

As the cousins obeyed the order, going into the centre of the barn, Jolly congratulated himself upon the way in which he was carrying out his superior's instructions. While desirous of vengeance, Duke had decided that it should be restricted to a severe beating with fists and feet. There must, he had stated, be no shooting as that would attract unwanted attention. So, with such a restriction placed upon him, Jolly had been determined to ensure that their victims were also denied the use of weapons. Satisfied that he had achieved his intentions, he was about to tell his men to do their work when he heard a soft footfall from his rear. While his men looked around, he kept his eyes to the front.

A small figure appeared in the main entrance. Bare-headed, he had short-cropped black hair and sallow, cheerful, Oriental features. He wore a loose fitting black cotton shirt, which was hanging outside trousers of the same material that were tucked into Hessian boots, and he was unarmed. Apart from the lack of a pigtail, he might have been a typical Chinese coolie, one of those who were already to be found in the United States.

'Devil-san!' the new arrival began, hurrying across the room and passing between Stone and Jolly. 'General Houston says for you to co—'

'Hold hard there, you yeller-skinned varmint!' Stone bellowed, shooting out his right hand to grasp the back of the small Oriental's shirt neck and starting to tug at it. 'Get the hell out of—'

As either Hardin or his cousin could have warned the burly man, such an action was ill-advised to say the least. While Tommy Okasi was undoubtedly of Oriental descent, he did not belong to the Chinese race. He was, in fact, Japanese and possessed a sturdy fighting spirit which the Chinese coolies, with whom Stone had been acquainted, only rarely exhibited.

Five years ago, a ship commanded by Hardin's father had come across a derelict vessel drifting in the China Sea. The only survivor had been Tommy Okasi, half dead, and with no possessions other than the clothing on his back, a pair of swords and the bow and quiver of arrows which were now leaning against his saddle. On recovering, he had proved to speak a little English. However, when questioned, he had given no explanation for his presence aboard the other vessel. Nor had he evinced any desire to return to his native land. Instead, he had stayed on in Captain Hardin's ship attaching himself to his rescuer's son. What was more, while he had a very thorough

36

knowledge of his nation's highly effective martial arts, he was content to act as Ole Devil Hardin's valet.

Even before the events which had caused Hardin and Mannen Blaze to leave Louisiana and join other members of the Hardin, Fog and Blaze clan in Texas, Tommy had been of great service to his employer. Since arriving and becoming involved in the struggle for independence, he had taken a full part in their activities and had shared their dangers.

All in all, Tommy Okasi – even without his two swords, which for some reason he was no longer wearing – was not the kind of man to be treated the way Stone was doing.

Feeling the hand take hold of his collar and himself being jerked roughly backwards, Tommy reacted with devastating speed. Instead of allowing himself to be flung by his captor and out of the door, he contrived to go towards Stone. The loose fit of his shirt did nothing to impede his movements. Twisting his torso to the left, he bent his right arm in front of him. Then, at exactly the crucial moment, he reversed his body's direction and propelled the arm to the rear.

'*Kiai!*' Tommy ejaculated, giving the traditional spiritual cry as he struck at his assailant.

To Stone, who had not expected such a display of aggression from a member of what he had always regarded as being a passive and easily bullied race, it seemed as if he had been kicked in the *solar plexus* by a mule. Releasing the collar, as all the breath was rammed from his body by the force of the impact, the burly man clutched at the stricken area and folded over. He retreated hurriedly a few steps, trying to replenish his lungs, before tripping and sitting down.

Having liberated himself, Tommy continued to move with rapidity and deadly purpose. Jolly's head had swivelled around as he heard Stone's agony-filled croak on being struck and the pistol's barrel wavered out of alignment. Before he could return it to its original point of aim, the small Oriental turned his unwanted attention upon him.

Around and up whipped Tommy's left arm. He did not strike with his clenched fist, but the result was just as effective. Keeping the fingers extended and together, with the thumb bent across his palm, he drove the hand so its edge passed under Jolly's chin and chopped into his prominent Adam's apple. Jolly might have thought himself fortunate had he known how effective the *tegatana*, hand sword, blow of *karate* could be, for he was just too far away to take it at full power. As it was, the result was not to be despised. To Jolly, it seemed that his windpipe had been assaulted by a blunt axe. Reeling backwards, making a sound like a chicken being strangled, he involuntarily tightened his right forefinger on the pistol's trigger. The hammer swung around, propelling the flint in its jaws against the steel frizzen which hinged forward allowing the sparks to fall on to the priming charge. A spurt of flame, passing through the touch-hole, ignited the powder in the chamber. With a crash and cloud of white smoke, the weapon fired. As its bullet flew harmlessly into the wall, the recoil snatched it from Jolly's grasp. Not that he gave its loss any thought. Staggering towards the wall, with hands clutching at his neck, his only interest was in trying to breathe.

'Get the bastards!' yelled Bellowes, the stocky townsman who had 'asked' for Duke's advice at the *cantina*.

'Know something, Cousin Devil?' Blaze inquired, sounding almost plaintive, as he watched two of the quartet reaching for the pistols in their belts as they all moved forward. 'I don't reckon they'll listen to reason.'

'I never thought they would' Hardin answered.

To give Lacey – the big, burly, buckskin-clad man who had 'protested' against Duke's criticism of Houston's policies – and Bellowes their due, they intended to use the firearms as clubs in accordance with Jolly's instructions. However, they found that doing so was far easier to plan than to carry out.

Timing his action perfectly, Hardin demonstrated his *savate* training by kicking Bellowes's hand as it was dragging the pistol free. Having done so, while Bellowes yelped with pain and dropped the pistol, Hardin turned on his second attacker, who was called Tate and who was dressed in a similar fashion to Stone. Ducking beneath the man's hands as they reached towards him, Hardin caught him around the knees and, straightening up, tossed him over to crash to the floor. Even as Hardin disposed of Tate, Bellowes retaliated by delivering a right cross to the jaw which sent him across the barn to collide with the burro.

Employing a rapidity of motion that was vastly different from the slothful manner in which he had been behaving up to that moment, Blaze gave his attention to Lacey. Bounding into range, the red head flung forward his knotted right fist. Carrying the full weight of his body behind them, his knuckles made

38

contact with the centre of Lacey's face. Despite having almost reached the end of its flight, the blow was still hard enough to make its recipient release the pistol, which had just come clear of his belt, and he lumbered backwards a few steps with blood flowing freely from his squashed nose.

Although the smallest of Duke's party, the fourth attacker did not hesitate to try to avenge Lacey. Dressed in the fashion of a French Creole dandy, McCann was a cocky young man who considered himself to be very tough. Catching Blaze's right shoulder, McCann tugged and, as he turned, drove a punch into his stomach. While the blow landed fairly hard, it made little or no impression upon the solid wall of muscle with which it had connected. Startled by the lack of distress which he had expected to cause, McCann sent his right fist after the left, and with as little effect.

Looking almost benevolently at his assailant, who seemed diminutive in comparison with his own bulk, Blaze shot out his hands. Alarm came to McCann's face as he felt the lapels of his jacket grasped and he was lifted from the floor as if he weighed no more than a baby. Then, as Lacey – who matched the red head in size – came back with the intention of repaying him for the blow to the nose, Blaze gave a heave and flung McCann aside. Although he alighted on his feet, the young man had no control over his movements. Unable to stop himself, he rushed onwards until he collided with and disappeared over the bales of hay behind which the two boys had hidden while eavesdropping upon Duke's instructions.

After having struck and disarmed Jolly, Tommy watched the attacks being made upon Hardin and Blaze. He was ready to go to either's aid if the need arose. Behind him, Stone lurched erect breathing heavily. Rubbing his torso where Tommy's elbow had impacted, the burly man moved forward. Hearing the other approaching, Tommy turned. He was only just in time, a huge hand was reaching for him. Before Stone's fingers could close on the small Oriental, he felt his wrist gripped with surprising strength and given a peculiar jerking twist. Just how it happened, Stone could never imagine, but the barn suddenly seemed to revolve as his feet left the floor and he sailed over Tommy's shoulder to land heavily on his back.

Still croaking hoarsely and having trouble breathing, Jolly had started to move in when he saw Stone rise. He was amazed to see his burly companion thrown with such ease, but, hoping to take Tommy by surprise, he charged forward. He met with no greater success than Stone, being treated to a similar *kata-seoi* shoulder throw and deposited almost on top of his companion. Having done so, Tommy darted away to help Hardin who was being attacked by Bellowes and Tate.

The fight continued to rage. It was fierce and hectic, but, despite their numerical superiority, far from satisfactory where Jolly's party were concerned. They had come to the barn expecting little difficulty in dealing with Hardin and Blaze. Instead, due to Tommy's intervention, their victims were able to turn the tables on them.

As when dealing with the Winglow brothers, Hardin relied upon his speed, agility and knowledge of *savate* to defend himself. Blaze lacked his cousin's qualities, but was stronger and just as able to take care of himself, using skill instead of relying upon brute strength. By far the smallest of any of the combatants, even McCann being taller, Tommy Okasi was anything but the least effective. His use of *ju jitsu* and *karate*, which were all but unknown in the Western World at that period,* more than off-set all the advantages his opponents had in the matter of size and weight.

Matched against three such talented performers, Jolly and his companions found themselves outclassed. In eight minutes, it was just about over. Having returned to the fray, McCann was put out of it when Hardin kicked him under the jaw. Shortly after, Blaze removed Lacey and Tate by coming up behind them while they were attacking his cousin, catching them by the scruff of their necks and banging their heads together. He had been free to do so because he had knocked Bellowes towards Tommy, who had deftly applied the finishing touch. A *nukite*, piercing hand – thrust into Bellowes' stomach folded him over so that Tommy could follow up with a *tegatana* chop to the base of the skull which dropped him as limp as a back-broke rabbit.

With all their companions sprawling unconscious, Jolly and Stone found themselves faced with the uninterrupted attentions of the two young men who should have been their victims. Both of them were soon being knocked around the barn, driven by Hardin's and Blaze's fists. While his cousin delivered a *coup-*

---

* Until the visits by Commodore Perry U.S.N.'s flotilla in 1853–54, there was little contact between Japan and the United States of America.

de-grace to Stone, Hardin caught Jolly with a left uppercut which flung him backwards through the door. Going out to make sure that the undertaker was finished, Hardin heard shouts and running footsteps. Halting, and ignoring Jolly as he lay supine and motionless, Hardin – who looked anything but tidy or dandified at that moment – turned to see who was coming.

In the lead, striding out angrily, his face registering extreme disapproval, was Colonel William Barrett Travis.

CHAPTER FOUR

A MISSION OF VITAL IMPORTANCE

'WITH respect, sir,' William Barrett Travis said, after having read the contents of the dispatch which had been received that afternoon and heard what the General Samuel Houston intended to do about it. 'I don't think that Captain Hardin is a suitable man to carry out such an important assignment.'

'Why not, Colonel?' Houston inquired.

Seated behind the desk of the big Spanish colonial style mansion which had been donated by its owner as Houston's headquarters whilst in San Antonio de Bexar, the commanding general of the Republic of Texas's army was an imposing and impressive figure. Big, thickset, with almost white hair, he had blue eyes that seemed strangely young in such a seamed, leathery and deeply tanned face. Although he would have preferred less formal garments, he was wearing the kind of uniform which the enlisted men expected of one with his exalted rank. The dark blue, close-buttoned, single-breasted coat had a high, stand-up collar. It was ornamented by gold shoulder scales, bearing the triple star insignia of a major general and by two rows of nine blind buttonholes in a 'herring-bone' pattern. He had a red silk sash around his waist, but his leather belt with a sabre hanging from its slings was on the hat-rack by the door, as was his black, bicorn chapeau. His tight-legged fawn riding breeches ended in black Wellington leg boots with spurs on their heels.

'If his behaviour since arriving in San Antonio is anything to go by,' Travis replied, looking straight to the front and ignoring the man who was sitting at his left, 'he's reckless, irresponsible and can't – or won't – avoid getting involved in fights no matter what duty he's supposed to be carrying out.'

'You know young Hardin, Jim,' Houston remarked, looking at the third occupant of the room. 'What do you say?'

'I can't deny that Devil gets into fights, Sam,' James Bowie admitted. 'He's a fighting man from soda to hock*—'

'That's as maybe, Colonel,' Travis interrupted. 'But an ability to get involved in brawls isn't what I'd regard as a desirable quality for the man the General needs. He has to take on a mission of vital importance.'

'I'm not gainsaying that,' Bowie answered, glancing with asperity at the other colonel. 'Devil might get into fights, but I've never known him to start one without good cause.'

'That depends on how you interpret good cause,' Travis countered coldly. 'From what I've been told, he became involved in the one at the *cantina* because he insisted that two men made room for him at the bar. In addition, not content with disabling them, he got himself into another fight, even though his man had come to tell him that the General wanted to see him.'

'Way I heard it,' Bowie objected, 'those fellers didn't give him any choice but to fight.'

'*He* started the one at the *cantina*,' Travis insisted. 'According to Sergeant Brill, he walked in and deliberately provoked those two men—'

'If he did, he must have had a damned sight better reason than just wanting to get through to the bar,' Bowie declared. 'And, as far as I know, 'nobody's got around to letting him tell his side of it as yet.'

Watching the two officers glowering at each other, Houston felt perturbed. He wondered if it would be wise to leave them together in San Antonio after the rest of the army had withdrawn to the east. Each in his own way was an excellent fighting man and a capable leader, but they had outlooks and natures which might prove to be incompatible. Their differences could easily damage the effectiveness with which they carried out their duty of defending the Alamo and, if possible, delaying Santa Anna for long enough to let Houston reorganize his forces ready to meet the Mexicans in battle.

'Suppose we ask him now, gentlemen?' Houston suggested, acting as peace-maker as he had had to do many times when there had been clashes of will or personalities between the leaders of his various regiments. 'Will you ask him to come in, Jim?'

* In the game of faro, the first card of the deck is called the 'soda' and the last is the 'hock'.

'Sure,' Bowie answered, coming to his feet and crossing the room.

Despite knowing that he had successfully completed a difficult and dangerous scouting mission, delivering much useful infirmation about the Mexican army's strength and progress, Ole Devil Hardin felt distinctly uneasy when Bowie opened the door of the study and passed on the General's summons.

Colonel Travis had been anything but pleased by the discovery that Hardin and his cousin, Mannen Blaze, had become involved in a second brawl and had rendered more members of the Republic of Texas' army unfit for duty. Nor had he been in any mood to listen to explanations, particularly when he had learned what had brought Tommy Okasi to the livery barn. Instead, Travis had suggested icily that the cousins would be advised to pay greater attention to their military duties and should reserve any further inclination for fighting for use against the Mexicans. Accepting the comments without argument, and not permitting Blaze – who was seething with indignation over what he regarded as Travis' unjust treatment – to speak up in his defense, Hardin had once again tidied himself up ready to report to Houston.

On Hardin's arrival at headquarters, he had been told that the General could not see him straight away. A messenger had brought in dispatches of considerable importance which required Houston's immediate attention. Before hurrying away, the General's aide – a harassed-looking young captain – requested that Hardin should remain in the hall until he was sent for. Returning with Bowie and Travis, the aide had taken them into the office. Taking note of Travis's cold scowl as he went by, Hardin could guess at the report which would be made regarding his activities. So he had misgivings when he was finally called in by Bowie.

Little of Hardin's perturbation showed as he went by Bowie, into the room and came under the scrutiny of the two senior officers. However, he was not as composed as he forced himself to appear. In fact, by the time he came to a halt in front of the desk he felt downright ill-at-ease, even though he was managing to conceal it. Standing at a stiff military brace which Travis would probably have approved of under other circumstances, he looked straight ahead. For all that he was conscious of Houston studying his bruised left cheek and swollen top lip.

After what seemed to the young man to be a very long time, Houston said in flat tones which told little of his feelings. 'I hear you've been in trouble this afternoon, Captain Hardin.'

'Yes, sir,' Hardin answered, allowing his gaze to drop to the speaker's tanned and expressionless face.

'On *two* occasions,' Houston went on, still giving no indication of how he felt about such conduct.

'Yes, sir,' Hardin agreed.

'Do you make a habit of picking fights?' Houston inquired.

'When it's necessary, sir,' Hardin replied respectfully.

'And you considered that it was necessary this afternoon?'

'Yes, sir.'

'Why?' Houston asked, glancing from Travis to Bowie who had returned and was standing alongside the straight-backed young man. 'You're at ease, captain.'

Relaxing slightly, Hardin explained how he had found the *Chicano* boy at the livery barn. Learning who had administered the beating and why, he had made his way to the *cantina* to investigate. Before going in, he had listened to the agitator answering questions and had taken notice of who was asking them.

Recognizing the threat to Houston's military strategy, Hardin had decided to intervene. However, he had known that to attempt anything in his official capacity would avail him nothing. Enlisted men in the Republic of Texas's army, being volunteers, were generally not so well disciplined that they would obey orders given by an officer who did not belong to their own respective regiments. What was more, his clan were known to be supporters of the General's policies. So the agitator and his assistants would know why he was interfering and would have resisted his attempts, which could have caused fighting to break out between the rest of the customers.

With those thoughts in mind, Hardin had formulated a plan which he had believed might serve his purpose. Identifying the *Chicano* boy's assailants and making an accurate assessment of their natures, he had approached them in a manner that was calculated to make them angry. He had been gambling that the rest of the customers would prefer to watch a fight than to sit listening to the agitator talking.

'I'd heard that Bill Cord always made anybody who was

spoiling for a fight take it outside,' Hardin concluded. 'And I figured that when he did, pretty near the whole of the crowd would follow us.'

There was a brief silence as the young man came to the end of his explanation. All the time he was talking, he was also watching the General. Not that the scrutiny had produced any result. Houston's leathery features had remained as impassive as if he had been one of the Cherokee Indians with whom he had lived for several years. However, Hardin had heard Bowie grunt appreciatively on two occasions and figured that there was at least one person in the room on his side. He had not attempted to look at Travis. Nor had he heard anything to indicate how the bow-necked colonel was responding to his story.

'You figured it right,' Bowie declared in a hearty and satisfied voice, turning his gaze to Travis. 'And I reckon we can be thankful that you did.' Then, seeing that the comment was puzzling Hardin, he continued, 'The other boy's daddy came to tell us what they'd heard, Devil, which's why Colonel Travis and I were headed for the *cantina*. Had an idea it might be as well to get the fellers out and away, only I reckoned we could have trouble in getting them to leave; especially the ones who weren't in our regiments and had been drinking. You getting them outside that way helped us do it, wouldn't *you* say, Colonel Travis?'

'It helped us,' Travis conceded almost grudgingly. 'But there was still the second fight.'

'There was no way we could have avoided it, sir,' Hardin stated politely. 'They were the agitator's men, the ones who'd helped him get the conversation going the way he wanted at the *cantina*. I recognized two of them and figured they weren't exactly coming to thank me.'

'What happened, Devil?' Bowie inquired, determined that the young man should be completely exonerated and that Travis should admit he was wrong.

'They pretended to think they'd caught us robbing the barn,' Hardin replied. 'Then the one who looked like an undertaker threw down on us with a pistol and made us shed our weapons—'

'You let them *disarm* you, knowing what they were going to do?' Travis asked.

'I thought that it was for the best, sir,' Hardin answered,

46

without showing any resentment over the interruption. 'Way we'd been acting, particularly cousin Mannen, they didn't have any notion that we knew who they really were and putting off our weapons clinched it. They were sure that we didn't suspect them. We were gambling on them not wanting to do any shooting as it would bring folks to see what was happening when what they wanted was to work us over with their fists.'

'There were still six of them against the two of you,' Travis pointed out, but there was a subtle change in his voice and it had become slightly less critical. 'I'd say they were very stiff odds, even without shooting.'

'Yes, sir,' Hardin conceded. 'But we'd lulled their suspicions and, with Cousin Mannen acting scared, they were likely to be over confident. Besides—'

'Go on,' Houston prompted, having observed the change in Travis' tone.

'I'd seen Tommy Okasi coming, sir,' Hardin obliged, wondering if he was winning the General over. There was nothing in his attitude to supply a clue, although Travis appeared to be softening a little. 'He could tell there was something wrong, so he made sure they didn't hear him until he was ready to let them. When he saw us dropping our weapons, he guessed what was going on and left his swords outside so that they would think he was harmless.' Try as he might, Hardin could not restrain a faint smile over the thought of how Stone, having fallen into the little Oriental's trap, was disillusioned. 'Which they did and that evened the odds up considerably.'

'There's others have made the mistake of thinking that little feller is harmless and come to regret it,' Bowie confirmed with a broad grin. 'You've never seen anything like the way he can fight, Sam. Fact being, those yahoos are lucky they didn't get hurt worse than they did.'

'Is that all, Captain Hardin?' Houston inquired, displaying no emotion at all. His face could have been a figure drawn upon a wooden fence.

'Yes, sir,' the young man replied, stiffening slightly as he realized that judgement would soon be upon him. 'I apologize for the delay in reporting to you—'

'Think nothing of it,' the General boomed, and he smiled broadly. 'I couldn't have seen you straight away if you had come and it sure as Sam Hill wasn't your fault that you got delayed.' His eyes swung to the seated colonel and he went on,

'He could have spent his time in worse ways, don't you think, Bill?'

'Well, sir,' Travis answered, his sense of fair play having caused him to revise his opinion of Hardin so that he eyed the young man with approbation. 'I don't approve officers being involved in brawls with the enlisted men, but I'm satisfied that it was justified on this occasion.'

'Thank you, sir,' Hardin ejaculated, showing his delight at having received what was tantamount to an apology and an accolade.

'You could have explained what started the fight when Colonel Travis questioned you outside the *cantina*, or at the barn,' Houston pointed out. 'It would have avoided any misunderstanding about your motives.'

'Yes, sir,' Hardin admitted, but tactfully decided against saying that he doubted whether Travis would have listened to an explanation in either instance. Instead, he went on, 'Like I said, the agitator had established his "right" to freedom of expression. So I figured that if he heard me explaining things to Colonel Travis after the fight, he might be able to use it against us. He could have said that one of your officers had picked on and hurt bad a couple of fellers rather than let him speak his piece. So I concluded it was better to keep quiet and explain in private.'

'Not every young man would have seen it in that light,' Houston praised.

'I must admit that I misjudged you, captain,' Travis declared, standing up. 'The circumstances of our meeting led me to assume that you were a reckless, hot-headed trouble-maker and finding you'd been in a second fight did nothing to change my opinion. I was wrong and I don't mind admitting it. You may have taken some chances, but they were calculated risks and not made recklessly.'

'Thank you, sir,' Hardin answered and he could not entirely hide his relief as he saw Houston nodding in agreement. 'Anyway, we came through it all right.'

'Which's more than can be said for that damned agitator's men,' Bowie remarked, showing his satisfaction over the way in which his protege had been exonerated. 'I don't reckon he'll be able to use any of them for a spell.'

'He's still around, sir,' Hardin warned. 'I could go—'

'You *could*,' Bowie grinned. 'But you're not going to. Don't

48

be a hawg, young Ole Devil, you've had your share of the fun. Leave us old timers have some.' His eyes turned to the general and he went on, 'If it's all right with you, Sam, I'll go and ask that feller if he'll head back and tell Johnson that we're happy with the way things are being run, but don't take kindly to folks trying to enlist men who're already serving.'

'Do that, Jim,' Houston confirmed, anger clouding his features for a moment. 'Damn Johnson—' Then the imperturbable mask returned and he looked at the other colonel. 'I can't see any objection to letting Captain Hardin take on the assignment, can you, Bill?'

'Not any more, sir,' Travis answered. 'If there's nothing further, I've duties which need my attention.'

'Go to them, Bill,' the General authorized. 'If the rifles arrive in time, I'll send some of them to you.'

'Thank you, sir,' Travis replied, although he, Houston and Bowie all realized that the Alamo Mission would most likely be under heavy siege before the weapons could reach it. He turned to the young man, whom he now regarded in a far more favourable light than when he had first entered the office, extending his right hand. 'Good luck, Captain Hardin. I won't advise you against getting involved in fights. Just keep on thinking before you do it.'

'I will, sir,' Hardin promised, shaking hands.

'I'll go too, Sam,' Bowie drawled. 'If that's all right with you.'

'Sure, Jim,' the General confirmed. 'Try to send that feller back to Johnson in one piece. I'd hate him to start thinking we'd got something against him and his men.'

'I'll do my level best,' Bowie grinned, then offered his right hand to Hardin for a warm and friendly shake. 'Good luck, young Ole Devil, in case I don't see you again before you pull out. Could be you'll need it before you're through with the assignment.'

Watching the two colonels turning from the desk, his fingers still tingling from Bowie's grip, Hardin wondered what kind of assignment he was to be given.

4

CHAPTER FIVE

À VERY DELICATE SITUATION

WHILE waiting until James Bowie and William Barrett Travis had left his office, Major General Samuel Houston studied the tall young man who was standing at the other side of the desk. Watching Ole Devil Hardin, and thinking of the assignment which he was to be asked to carry out, the General liked what he saw.

That had not been the case when Hardin first entered the room. Seeing him then, the General had been inclined to accept Colonel Travis's assessment of his character. However, as the interview had progressed, Houston had revised his opinion. Despite the way in which he had walked, with a free-striding, straight-backed confidence that came close to being a swagger, he was anything but a strutting, self-important and over-prideful hot-head who relied upon family influence to carry him through any difficulties that he himself had created by his attitude and behaviour. It was, the General had concluded, the beard and moustache more than anything which gave his Mephistophelian features an aspect of almost sinister arrogance.

On the other hand, Houston conceded that Hardin was no Hamlet filled with gloomy foreboding, misgivings or doubts when faced with the making of a decision. Behind the externals, there was a shrewd, capable reliability. As he had proved since his arrival in San Antonio and – if the report of his scouting mission was any criterion – on other occasions, when he found a situation which required immediate attention, he was willing to act upon his own initiative. What was more important, to Houston's way of thinking, he was prepared to stand by the consequences of his actions.

The latter had been apparent as Hardin had been facing the inquiry into his conduct that afternoon. While he had been somewhat perturbed on entering the office, he had hidden it very well. Yet, even though he had known he had acted for the best of reasons and had achieved his purpose under difficult and dangerous conditions, he had not tried to carry off the affair with a high hand. Nor had he counted upon his not unimportant family connections with Houston or Bowie to gain him automatic absolution. Instead, showing no resentment towards Travis's hostile attitude, he had explained his reasons with a polite modesty which had commanded the General's respect.

Summing up his impressions, Houston decided that young Ole Devil Hardin was brave without being foolhardy. He could think not only for the present but also for the future. That had been proven by his reason for not having explained why he had been fighting in front of the *cantina* when by doing so he might have gained exculpation and Travis's approbation. With such qualities, he would be the ideal man for the important mission.

What was more, the General felt sure that Hardin – provided he survived – could become a figure of considerable importance and a guiding hand in the affairs of Texas, whether it became an independent republic or one of the United States of America.

'Sit down, Captain,' Houston drawled, as the door closed. He pushed the humidor across the desk after raising its lid. 'Help yourself to a smoke.'

'Thank you, sir,' Hardin replied, taking the chair which Travis had occupied and helping himself to a cigar. Then he winced a little and gave his right side a gentle rub.

'Are you all right, boy?' Houston inquired solicitously and his concern was only partly motivated by the possibility of the younger man being unable to carry out the mission.

'Just a mite sore, sir,' Hardin replied with a wry grin.

'Would you like a drink to soothe it away?' Houston asked. His face took on an appreciative expression and he stamped on the floor. 'Don Sebastian keeps a good cellar and he's given me the use of it. I'll soon have something brought up if you're so minded.'

Although the General did not know it, his words were the cause of consternation to a man in the wine cellar. Short, plump, middle-aged and wearing the white clothing of a Mexican house servant, he was kneeling on the top of one of the wine racks. He held a glass tumbler with its bottom to his right ear. The upper end was pressed against the ceiling, which was also the floor of the study.

The Latin temperament had always been highly susceptible to intrigue, and the wine-rack being used by the man was sited to allow eavesdropping on private and confidential conversations in the study. Don Sebastian Carillo de Biva had had that in mind when turning over his mansion to be used as Houston's headquarters. A wealthy land owner, de Biva was running with the hare and hunting with the hounds. So, although he was giving his support to the Texians, he had also allowed his *major domo* to organize a spy ring with which to supply information to the Mexicans. By having done so, he hoped to emerge from the present situation no worse off than he had been before the declaration of independence whichever side should be the victors.

De Biva and his family were no longer at the mansion, having moved west to their *hacienda* in what would later become the American State of New Mexico and which was not involved in the Texians' bid for freedom. Staying behind, the *major domo*, Juan Juglares, had put his knowledge of the premises to good use. He spoke English far better than he admitted and, by listening from the top of the wine-rack, had already been successful in his spying task.

Having noticed the excitement caused by the arrival of a dispatch rider, Juglares had sensed that something of more than usual importance was in the air. So he had come to the wine cellar and taken up his position. From various comments that he had overheard between Houston, Bowie and Travis, he realized that the matter under discussion was likely to prove well worth the risks of listening. He had no wish to be driven from his point of vantage while there was still more to be learned.

'Not for me, thank you, sir,' Hardin replied, much to Juglares' relief.

'Have it your own way, boy,' Houston drawled and indicated a sheet of paper which was lying on the desk. 'Let's get down to business. You'll most likely know why Stephen Austin's Commission went to New Orleans, seeing that your Uncle Marsden was one of the Commission.'

'Yes, sir,' Hardin agreed. 'To try and recruit men, obtain weapons and generally raise support for our cause. That's pretty common knowledge, sir.'

'Too common,' Houston grunted, and went on as the younger

man stiffened. 'I'm not blaming Marsden for *that*, boy. We never tried to keep it a secret.'

'Is that a report on how they're getting on, sir?' Hardin inquired, relaxing as he saw that his uncle was not being held responsible for disclosing the purpose of the Commission.

'It is.'

'Are they being successful?'

'To a certain degree, although they're having some difficulties. However, they have obtained five hundred new caplock rifles and ten thousand rounds of ready-made ammunition for them and are arranging for them to be shipped to us.'

'Five hundred *caplock* rifles?' Hardin repeated eagerly. 'That's *bueno*, sir. We can really make use of them.'

'I see that you're one who doesn't have any doubts about the caplock system,' Houston remarked.

There was considerable controversy between the adherents of the flintlock and the newer caplock mechanisms as a means of discharging a firearm.

'I don't, sir,' Hardin confirmed, and indicated the weapon in the loop on his belt. 'This Manton* pistol of mine's percussion-fired.'

'But not your rifle?'

'It is too, sir, in a way. You see I use what Uncle Ben Blaze calls a 'slide repeating' rifle. He bought it from some feller called Jonathan Browning† while he was up in Illinois last fall. Way I see it, though, the caplock's going to replace the flintlock completely. It's more certain, easier to load – I'm sorry, sir, but I feel strongly about it. In my opinion, for what it's worth, five hundred caplocks are worth double their number of flintlocks; particularly in wet weather.'

'You don't have to persuade *me*,' Houston stated with a grin. 'Some of us worn-out old fogies can see the advantages of the caplock as well as you smart young men.'

'I'm sorry, sir,' Hardin apologized.

Down in the cellar, Juglares moved restlessly and wished that the men above him would get down to business. Every

* Joseph 'Old Joe' Manton, gunsmith of London, England, an early maker of percussion-fired weapons.

† Jonathan Browning, gunsmith father of master firearms' designer, John Moses Browning. John Moses appears in: *Calamity Spells Trouble.*

minute he remained in such a compromising position increased his chances of being caught. Retribution would be swift and final if that should happen.

'Anyway, boy,' Houston went on, waving aside the apology. 'They'll be at Santa Cristobal Bay, that's about ten miles north of the Matagorda Peninsula, in seven days. You'll collect them from the ship and deliver them to me at Washington-on-the-Brazos, or wherever I might be at the time.'

'Seven days, sir?' Hardin repeated, thinking about the distances involved and the type of terrain which he would have to traverse. 'How long will the ship wait?'

'No more than two days, and it will only run into the Bay at night. While we're in control pretty well from the Brazos to the coast, there's the Mexican Navy to be taken into consideration. They've a frigate blockading Galveston, with a ten-gun brig patrolling between it and Matamoros. So the captain daren't hang around in the vicinity for too long. It's vitally important that the shipment doesn't fall into Santa Anna's hands.'

'I can see that, sir. Those five hundred caplocks and their ammunition—'

'It goes much deeper than that, boy,' Houston interrupted. 'In fact, it could have an adverse effect upon any future supplies and aid from the United States. We're involved in a very delicate situation. As I said, we didn't try to keep the Commission's purpose a secret. Santa Anna found out what we were hoping to do. So his consul in New Orleans and the Mexican Ambassador up at Washington, D.C., are raising all manner of protests over it.'

'That's only to be expected, sir,' Hardin pointed out philosophically. 'But it won't stop our kin and friends back in the United States from helping us.'

'It might,' Houston corrected. 'There's considerable opposition from the anti-slavery faction to any suggestion that, after we've won our independence, Texas should be considered for annexation by the United States. Their contention is that by allowing that to happen it might result in the formation of further 'slave' States.* Rather than have that happen they'd sooner see Texas remain under Mexican rule. So they're de-

* The Texians had suggested that, after annexation, in view of the vast area of land which would be involved, Texas could be divided into three or four separate States.

manding that the United States refuses to allow even private support or aid for us.'

'But surely we've our own supporters in Congress, sir,' Hardin protested.

'We have,' Houston conceded. 'And they'd be willing to stand by us more openly if it was only the Mexicans and the anti-slavery faction involved. But Santa Anna's made representations to various European countries. He's claiming that our "rebellion", as he calls it, is preventing him from bringing about settled conditions which will allow expansion, development and overseas trade. As the Europeans are interested in the latter, seeing a chance of profit, they are taking the line that the United States has no right to interfere in the domestic problems of another country. So far our supporters in Congress have been able to evade the issue by pointing out that there is no proof that aid has been given since the declaration of independence.'

'And the shipment would furnish that proof, sir,' Hardin said quietly.

'It would,' Houston confirmed. 'It's true that the arms were donated by private individuals and have nothing to do with Congress, or the United States, but it will embarass our supporters and lessen their chances of winning the annexation issue. So you can see why it's very important that the shipment doesn't fall into the Mexicans' hands. If it does, there will be pressure put on Congress to stop *all* aid.'

Crouching on the wine-rack, ignoring the ache in his legs and neck, Juglares was congratulating himself. What he had heard was of the greatest importance. Not even the discovery that Bowie and Travis were going to hold the Alamo Mission had been of such value. While his first inclination was to leave immediately and arrange for the information to be passed on without delay, he refrained. The more he could learn, the greater use it would be.

'Even granting the extra two days, sir,' Hardin said, after a few seconds' thought. 'That doesn't leave me much time to have Company "C" join me from the regiment, then get to Santa Cristobal Bay. Particularly taking along wagons to carry the shipment.'

'It doesn't,' Houston admitted. 'Especially as the longer the ship is delayed, the greater chance of it being captured. There's one thing, though, you won't be using wagons. Like you said, they'd slow you down too much. Mules're faster and better suited to the kind of country you'll be covering.'

'That's true enough, sir. But do we have enough of them available?'

'Ewart Brindley does. Do you know him?'

'I've never met him, sir. But I've heard tell of him—'

'And most of what you've heard is true,' Houston said with a grin, having noticed the inflexion in the younger man's voice. 'Old Ewart's just about as ornery and cross-grained a cuss as ever drew breath or drank corn liquor; but there's no better hand at working a mule train.'

'That's what I've always heard, sir,' Hardin answered.

'And that's one of the reasons I'm sending *you*, boy,' Houston went on. 'Your Uncle Edward has already spoken highly of your ability to get along with people. You'll have to handle Ewart real carefully though, even with the letter I'll be giving you for him. It's no good going along and expecting him to doff his hat, touch his forelock, say "Yes sir, captain," and take your orders. He's too cantankerous for that and, the way he sees it, as they're *his* mules, neither you, I, nor anybody else can tell him how to use them.'

'There's some might say that it's his duty to use them, sir,' Hardin commented.

'If they did say it, he'd tell them to go straight to hell and take their notions of duty with them.'

'Isn't he for the Republic, sir?'

'Old Ewart's never been *for* anything in his whole life,' Houston warned with a grin. 'He's always *against*. Bear that in mind when you get to his place at Gonzales and you'll get along fine.'

'Will he be there, sir?' Hardin inquired.

'Di sent word he would be, getting everything ready to fall back with us.'

' "Di", sir?'

'Ewart's granddaughter. Her name's Charlotte Jane Martha, but I wouldn't advise you to call her any one of them. He's reared her since the Kiowas killed her momma and daddy back in 'Twenty-Two. They do say she can throw a diamond hitch faster, tighter and better than any man. That's where the "Di" comes from. Old Ewart thinks the world of her. So if you can get her on your side, that'll be as good as half the battle.'

'I'll keep it in mind, sir,' Hardin promised.

'You do that, boy,' Houston ordered, but in a friendly manner. 'Now, about an escort. I can get you as many men as you think you'll need from one or other of the outfits who're in town.'

'I'd sooner not do that, sir,' Hardin objected. 'For one thing I'd rather not be using men I don't know and who don't know me. And, anyway, to get them we'd have to explain to their officers why they're wanted. I think the fewer who know about the shipment the better. There's less chance of word getting to the Mexicans that way.'

'I'll go along with you on that, boy,' Houston conceded, nodding his approval. 'So far, at this end only you, Colonels Travis, Bowie and I know about it. And they don't know when or where it's due to arrive.'

'In that case, sir, I'd rather not take an escort from town. It would attract too much attention. From all I've heard, Ewart Brindley and his muleteers are pretty tough *hombres*.'

'They are,' the General confirmed. 'They've taken mule trains through Indian country more than once and come back with their hair.'

'Which means they can hold up their end, comes shooting,' Hardin said with satisfaction. 'If it's all right with you, sir, I'll not take an escort from town.'

At that moment, Juglares heard the handle of the cellar door being turned. With a surge of alarm he realized that whoever was outside would be able to enter. Such was his eagerness to overhear as much as possible of the General's conversation, that, on arriving, he had merely closed the door behind him—

And had left the key in the lock!

Even as the door began to creep slowly open, Juglares acted with commendable speed. He knew that he could not stay where he was and hope to remain undetected. Although it was late afternoon, the window in the outside trapdoor – through which barrels of wine were lowered into the cellar – was still letting in too much light. Nor could he think of any acceptable reason for being on top of the rack and the tumbler might give away his true purpose.

Swiftly, but quietly, Juglares rolled across the rack and lowered himself to the floor with it between him and the door. Having achieved this without making enough noise to betray himself, he peered between two of the shelves to find out who had disturbed him.

57

The intruder proved to be a thin, sharp-featured infantry soldier. Before entering, he looked back into the basement in a furtive manner. Apparently satisfied that he was not being observed, he advanced, subjecting the cellar to a similar cautious scrutiny. His whole attitude implied that he was not carrying out any official, or even lawful duty.

For a moment Juglares thought of remaining in concealment and allowing the soldier to do whatever he had come for and then depart. However, he saw the objections to such a course. Having stolen some of the liquor, which was almost certainly his reason for visiting the cellar, the soldier might lock the door on leaving. While Juglares could still escape by the trapdoor, the grounds were heavily guarded and he would be in plain view of a sentry. Of course, as *major domo*, he had every right to be in the cellar; although he would have to think up an explanation for making his exit that way instead of through the basement.

The decision was taken out of Juglares's hands.

'Hey!' yelped the soldier, coming to a halt and staring at the rack behind which the *major-domo* was standing. He seemed to be on the verge of turning and dashing out of the cellar. 'Who-all's there?'

'Only me, *senor*,' Juglares answered in soothing tones and, knowing that to do anything else would be futile and would arouse the other's suspicions, he walked from his place of concealment. 'Can I help you?'

'Who're you and what're you doing down here?' the soldier demanded, but his voice lacked the authority of one who had the right to be asking such a question.

'I am Don Sebastian Carillo de Biva's *major domo, senor*,' Juglares said, adopting his most imposing tone and manner. 'It is one of my duties, particularly in Don Sebastian's absence, to take care of the wine cellar.'

'It is, huh?' the soldier grunted, sounding impressed but still dubious and suspicious.

'*Si, senor*,' the *major domo* confirmed and went on craftily, 'If you wish, we can go and see the first sergeant. He will tell you who I am.'

The gamble paid off.

'Shucks, there ain't no call for that, *amigo*,' the soldier said hurriedly, just as Juglares had believed that he would. 'I've been sent down for a couple of bottles of whiskey, if you've got

58

'em. So if you'll give 'em to me, I'll get going and leave you to your work.'

'Certainly, *senor*,' the *major domo* replied. 'Don Sebastian keeps whiskey for his Texian friends. I will get it for you. Will two bottles be enough?'

'Well,' the soldier began, his eyes taking on an avaricious glint. 'The cap'n did say three now I come to think back on it.'

'Three it is, *senor*,' Juglares declared without hesitation.

Walking to the rack in which the bottles of whiskey were stored, the *major domo* felt relieved and cheerful. He was sure that the soldier had lied to him, but he did not care. The information he had already garnered was worth far more than the three bottles he had been asked for. Once he had handed them over, the *gringo* would go. What was more, he would be unlikely to mention that he had found anybody in the cellar as he should not have been there himself. When the soldier had left, Juglares hoped to resume the eavesdropping and find out if there was anything else to be learned.

Before the *major domo* could take out the first bottle, he heard heavy and authoritative footsteps descending the stairs and crossing the basement. So did the soldier and an expression of consternation came to his face. It grew rather than diminished as the burly figure of First Sergeant Gladbeck loomed through the open door.

'What's all this?' boomed the non-com, looking from the soldier to Juglares and back.

'I heard a noise in here and come to see who it was, serge,' the soldier answered. 'Found this feller here. He allows it's all right for him.'

'It is,' Gladbeck stated, having recognized and identified the Mexican. 'But you'd best get going afore I grow all suspicious and ask what you was doing down here in the first place.'

'Sure, serge,' the soldier replied and scuttled hurriedly away.

'What was he after, liquor?' the first sergeant inquired, turning his attention to Juglares.

'*Si senor*,' the *major domo* agreed. 'He said he'd been sent to collect three bottles of whiskey.'

'Three, now that's what I call being greedy,' Gladbeck grinned. 'Have you got everything you need for tonight? The General's entertaining his senior officers to dinner, there'll be eight of them.'

59

Since the non-com's arrival, Juglares had been thinking fast and had revised his line of action. While he had hoped to continue listening to what was said in the General's office, he had now decided against taking the chance. He already knew when and where the shipment of arms would arrive, that the officer charged with receiving it would go first to the town of Gonzales, and that he did not consider it necessary to take a military escort. Such information was far too valuable for him to risk being caught eavesdropping. What was more, he had just been given a perfect excuse for leaving the mansion and passing on his findings.

'Eight extra, *senor*,' the *major domo* said doubtfully. 'In that case, I'll have to go into town and make some purchases.'

As Juglares and the first sergeant left the cellar, Ole Devil Hardin was finishing outlining his plans for the collection of the shipment. Houston agreed that, as only he and the young man were aware of the date and place where it would arrive, the line of action which had been proposed stood every chance of succeeding.

CHAPTER SIX

I'D HATE TO GET KILLED

ALTHOUGH the rain had ceased to fall about half an hour earlier, Ole Devil Hardin and Tommy Okasi were still wearing the waterproof *ponchos* which they had donned to keep their clothing, saddles and other equipment as dry as possible. The moon had broken through the clouds and its pallid light was sufficient for the two young men to make out some details of the small hamlet at which they were intending to spend the night.

Having followed General Samuel Houston's advice and allowed their horses to rest at Shelby's Livery Barn overnight, Ole Devil and Tommy had left San Antonio de Bexar early that morning. Instead of accompanying them, Mannen Blaze had returned to the Texas Light Cavalry so that he could take command of Company 'C' during his cousin's absence.

Ole Devil had had no idea that his conversation with the General had been overheard and reported to the enemy. Nor did he suspect that plans were already in motion to circumvent him on the assignment, but he and Tommy were too experienced as campaigners to ride along the main trail which connected San Antonio and Gonzales.

All of the Mexican army's garrisons might have been driven out of Texas, but that did not mean military activity was at an end. Some of Santa Anna's volunteer cavalry regiments, the Rancheros Lancers for example, were comprised of *Creole* hacienda* owners' sons and their *vaqueros*. Hard-riding, tough and capable fighting men, they were sufficiently enterprising to carry out raids north of the Rio Grande. There were also groups of *Chicanos* who supported *el Presidente* and were always ready to strike at any unwary Texians with whom they came into contact. In addition, marauding bands of *Comancheros* and white renegades roamed in search of loot and plunder.

* Creole; a Mexican of pure Spanish blood.

61

Any such foes could be expected to watch a trail that carried traffic between two fair-sized towns. So, even though they had not been able to make such good time, Ole Devil and Tommy had ridden parallel to, but out of sight of it. That meant they were approaching the hamlet from across country. With the wind blowing from the east, the scent of them and their horses was being carried way from the buildings. Due to the rain, the ground was soft and their mounts' hooves were making little noise.

'There're some horses in the lean-to at the back of the *cantina!*' Ole Devil warned quietly, bringing his linebacked dun gelding to a halt about two hundred yards from the nearest building. 'But the rest of the town looks deserted.'

'Perhaps they belong to some of the men who have stayed behind to guard their homes,' Tommy suggested, stopping his bay gelding. His sibilant tones were no louder than those of his companion. 'Or they could be a patrol who have taken shelter from the rain.'

The two young men were not worried by the deserted aspect of the town. They found that less disturbing than the presence of the horses. On passing through while going to report to General Houston, they had found its population on the point of leaving for the greater security offered by the larger town of Guadalupe.

'It could be either,' Ole Devil agreed. 'But, if it is a patrol, is it from our army or Santa Anna's?'

'A wise man would make sure before letting them know he is close by,' Tommy pointed out.

'You're riding with a wise man, believe it or not,' Ole Devil declared, swinging to the ground and removing his hat. 'I'll drift on over and take a look.'

While Tommy was dismounting, Ole Devil hung his hat by its *barbiquejo* chin strap on the saddlehorn and strugged off his *poncho*. Folding and tucking it between the cantle and his bed roll, he removed the powder horn and bullet pouch which were slung across his shoulders and suspended them from the hilt of his sabre. There was an oblong leather pouch attached to his belt in the centre of his back. Although it held the means to load his rifle, he left it in place. To have removed it would have entailed drawing the belt through the loops of his breeches and the slot of the pistol's carrier. He had not worn the pouch in

San Antonio, but had fixed it into position before leaving that morning.

During the removal of these items which would be an encumbrance to swift and silent movement, the young Texian was examining the hamlet on the off chance that he might discover something to supply a clue to the identities of the horses' owners. He failed to do so, but did not advance immediately. Instead, he waited while his companion prepared to cover him as he was carrying out the scouting mission.

When the rain had started, Tommy had removed the string from his bow to prevent it from getting wet. The six foot long weapon – which had its handle set two-thirds of the way down the stave instead of centrally, as was the case with Occidental bows – was hanging in two loops attached to the left side of his saddle's skirts. To keep the flights of the his arrows dry, he had suspended the quiver from the saddlehorn and covered them with his *poncho*.

Allowing his horse to stand ground-hitched by its dangling, split-ended reins, Tommy duplicated Ole Devil's actions by removing hat and *poncho*. Then he retrieved his quiver and swung it across his back so that the flights of the arrows rose above his right shoulder and would be readily available to his 'draw' hand. With that done, he restrung the bow and nocked an arrow to the shaft.

'Are you taking your rifle?' Tommy inquired, when his companion made no attempt to pull the weapon from its saddle-boot.

'I can move faster and quieter without it,' Ole Devil replied and nodded to the bow. 'If you *have* to use that heathen device, try not to stick the arrow in my butt end will you?'

'I'll try,' Tommy promised, grinning as he heard what had come to be the usual comment under such circumstances.

Despite his remark, the Texian had complete confidence in his companion's ability as an archer. It was, in fact, very comforting to know that Tommy was ready to cover him if it should prove necessary. While the odds were in favour of the horses behind the *cantina* being owned by friends, Ole Devil did not discount the possibility that they might belong to enemies. If so, and if he got into some kind of trouble, he might need all the help he could get.

Tommy might be small, but Ole Devil knew he was

63

completely reliable. He was as deadly effective with the bow as he was with the *daisho*, the matched pair of slightly curved, long hilted swords which he carried; the thirty inch long *tachi* hanging by the slings at the left side of his belt and the eighteen inch blade *wakizashi* dangling on the right.*

Walking forward with his eyes continually raking the buildings for any sign of danger, Ole Devil found himself revising his opinion regarding the wind being from the west. Earlier he had cursed it when it had occasionally contrived to send some of the rain down the back of his neck. Now he had to admit that it was coming from an advantageous quarter. It was not carrying their scent to the horses behind the *cantina* nor had it caused their mounts to become aware of the other animals.

Leaving his big bowie knife sheathed and the Manton pistol in its belt-loop, Ole Devil drew nearer to the lean-to without being challenged. Aware of the danger, he took precautions against startling the horses. Hissing gently through his teeth, he alerted them to his presence and arrived without causing them to take fright and betray him. After giving his surroundings a thorough scrutiny and satisfying himself that he was not being watched by the owners of the animals, he stepped underneath the roof.

'Easy now, boy,' Ole Devil breathed, going up to the nearest horse in a calm and unhurried manner. Laying his left hand gently on its flank, he stoked it and went on, 'You're cool now, but I'd say you were out in the rain for a time.'

Having made this deduction, the Texian turned his attention to the horse's saddle. It was still in place, with the single girth† tight enough for the animal to be ridden. The large horn and bulging fork wooden tree covered by sheep-vellum and lined with wool, to which the girth and stirrup leathers were attached by simple straps, was typically Mexican in origin.

However, on going to the next animal, Ole Devil found that it was carrying a different kind of rig. Even before the conflict of interests had caused hostility towards the Mexicans, Texian saddlers had begun to develop their own type of horse's equipment. They were already producing a saddle with a smaller

* The *wakizashi* was traditionally carried thrust through the girdle, but Tommy Okasi had had his fitted with belt slings since arriving in the United States.

† Due to its Mexican connotations, Texians rarely used the word 'cinch'.

horn, little swelling at the pommel, a very deep seat, wide fenders to the stirrups and double girths. The horse was fitted with such a rig and, like all the others, had a bed roll strapped to the cantle.

Continuing with his investigation, Ole Devil discovered one more Texas 'slick fork'. The other three horses had on double girthed rigs, but with a quilted, hammock-type seat and no horn, of the style made popular around 1812 in the Eastern United States by James Walker, a Philadelphia saddler. Unfortunately, the diversity of types supplied little or no information regarding the identities of the men who had ridden on them.

Standing by the last horse he had examined, Ole Devil was able to see into the alley which separated the *cantina* from its neighbouring building. Although the rear of the *cantina* was as dark and apparently deserted as the rest of the hamlet, there was a glow of light from the side window.

Leaving the lean-to, the Texian crossed to the alley in the hope that he might gain more information silently he crept forward, halting to peer cautiously around the side of the window. The light was supplied by a single lamp which was standing on a table in the centre of the room. Of the four men who were sitting at the table, one was a tall, slim *vaquero* whose *charro* clothing showed signs of hard travelling. The rest were hard-faced, unshaven white men dressed in buckskins. Yet another *gringo* was standing behind the bar cutting up pemmican. There were four flintlock rifles leaning against the counter.

Crouching below the level of the windowsill, Ole Devil went by and reached the front of the building. Instead of turning the corner, he looked around it cautiously. Nursing a rifle, a fifth man was sitting on a chair by the door.

Even as Ole Devil looked, the man lurched to his feet!

Although the young Texian felt sure that he had not been detected, he instinctively drew back his head. There was no outcry, nor anything else to suggest that he had been seen. For all that, without conscious thought, his right hand went to the most suitable weapon for his purpose in case the man should prove to be an enemy and come to investigate whatever he might have seen.

With that in mind, Ole Devil did not reach for his Manton pistol. Instead, his fingers enfolded the concave ivory handle of the bowie knife. Under the circumstances, it would be more

5   65

effective than the firearm and would not cause a general alarm. Weighing forty-three ounces, the knife's eleven-inch long, two-and-a-quarter-inches wide, three-eighths of an inch thick blade, and the scolloped brass butt cap, made it as good a club as a cutting and thrusting implement.

There was, Ole Devil told himself, no real reason for him to be taking such precautions. While the men were dirty, unshaven and not very prepossessing, they were not especially different from many members of the Republic of Texas's army which, in general, was more concerned with fighting efficiency than in trying to present a smart and military appearance. Nor was finding a *vaquero* with the buckskin-clad white men cause for alarm. Several regiments, Bowie's Texas Volunteers in particular, had *Chicanos* serving in their ranks.

Despite that, the young Texian felt uneasy. Try as he might, he could not think of any reason why he should be; but the feeling persisted.

After about thirty seconds had gone by without the man approaching the corner, Ole Devil once again surreptitiously peeped around. The man was now standing at the edge of the sidewalk and looking to the west along the trail. Then, making a gesture of impatience, he turned and stalked towards the *cantina* without so much as a glance in the young Texian's direction.

'Ain't no sign of him, Sid,' Ole Devil heard the man saying in protesting tones and a Northern accent as he went through the door which had been broken open. 'I bet he's holed up some place out of the rain and'll be staying there until morning.'

'Get the hell back out there and keep watch in case he ain't!' roared a second voice which had a harsh New England timbre. 'I want to be ready for him if he comes.'

Turning before the man reappeared, Ole Devil withdrew along the alley. He went as silently as he had come and just as carefully. Bending as he reached the window, he passed without attempting to look in. Then he straightened up and strode out faster. On coming into sight, he signalled for his companion to wait and hurried to rejoin him.

'There are six of them, Tommy,' Ole Devil reported *sotto voce*, and he described what he had seen, concluding, 'I'm damned if I know what to make of them, except that they're definitely not men from the town acting as guards. All I know is that I don't like the look of them.'

66

Neither Ole Devil nor Tommy attached any significance to the fact that two of the white men spoke with Northern accents. They knew that not all Texians had originated in the Southern States.

'They are waiting for somebody?' Tommy remarked.

'From what was said,' Ole Devil agreed. 'Just one man, the way they were talking.'

'Then, as they haven't unsaddled their horses, they may be expecting to move on when he joins them,' Tommy suggested. 'We could stay here and wait to see if they do.'

'Trouble being, if he has taken shelter from the rain and is staying there for the night, they'll not be leaving,' Ole Devil argued. 'Then again, they're not trying to hide the fact that they're in the *cantina*. If they were, they wouldn't be showing a light.'

'That doesn't mean they are friendly,' Tommy pointed out. 'They would know a light would lure anybody who was passing.'

'I'm not gainsaying it.'

'Then what shall we do?'

'I hate puzzles, Tommy,' Ole Devil replied. 'So I'm just naturally bound to get an answer to this one. Thing is, I'd hate to get killed before we've collected those rifles. General Sam and Uncle Edward'll be riled at me if I do. So as we can't play it safe we'll have to handle it sneaky.'

'Very wise old Nipponese saying, which I've just made up, says, "Always better to be sure than sorry",' Tommy announced soberly. 'What do you intend to do, Devil-san?'

Despite the light-hearted comments, neither Ole Devil nor Tommy was forgetting that they were engaged upon a mission of considerable importance. However, they also realized it was their duty to try and learn who the men might be and what they were doing in the hamlet. It only remained for them to decide how they might most safely satisfy their curiosity.

'I'll take both horses and swing around so that I ride into town along the trail from the east,' the Texian answered. 'You go through the alley on foot and be ready to cut in if there's trouble.'

'I expected that if there was walking, humble Nipponese gentleman would have to do it,' Tommy sighed with mock resignation, watching his companion gathering up the horses' reins.

'If you're *that* humble, you shouldn't be riding in the first place,' said Ole Devil and swung astride his tall, line-backed dun gelding. He started it moving and the no-smaller bay followed in response to his gentle tug on the reins. '*Sayonara.*'

'Remember old Nipponese proverb, which I've just made up,' Tommy counselled. ' "In time of war, wise man treats all others as enemies until they have proved differently".'

'I'll bear it in mind,' Ole Devil promised and caused the horses to move faster.

Keeping the arrow nocked to his bow's string, Tommy set off to carry out his part of the plan. Before he had reached the lean-to, he could neither see nor hear Ole Devil and the horses. Which proved to be fortunate.

The sound of footsteps on the planks of the sidewalk in front of the *cantina* reached the little Oriental's ears. Darting to the lean-to, he halted behind its back wall. So quietly had he been moving, even during the last brief dash, that the horses were unaware of his presence and he did not disturb them.

Two of the buckskin-clad white men, each carrying his rifle, came along the alley. However, Tommy had already attained his place of concealment and he listened to what they were saying as they approached.

'You reckon we'll come across him, Al?' asked one of the men, almost petulantly, his voice suggestive of a Northern origin. 'It's out of his way if he's going to—'

'I know it is,' the second interrupted and he too did not sound like a Southron. 'But we were told's he'd be heading for Gonzales first and this's the trail's goes to there. So we'll ride out for a couple of miles and see if there's any sign of him. If there ain't, we'll come back and see what Halford wants us to do.'

'But if he's holed up, he won't be along until after daylight,' the first man protested. 'And I don't cotton to the notion of hanging around here after sun up.'

By that time, the pair had reached the lean-to. Tommy was hoping to find out who they were looking for, but did not. The conversation was terminated as they collected their horses. Leading the animals outside, they mounted and rode away to disappear into the alley at the opposite end of the *cantina*. Tommy clicked his tongue impatiently over his failure to learn anything. Even the fact that the man did not wish to be in the hamlet during the daytime proved nothing. He might be a loyal

Texian who believed, like Ole Devil and Tommy, that the trail and locality could become unhealthy due to enemy raiders.

Waiting until the sounds of the two horses had faded into the distance, Tommy walked from behind the lean-to and into the alley. He adopted similar tactics to those used by Ole Devil as he came to the window. Holding his bow and arrow, low, he looked in. The Mexican and two of the white men were now standing at the customers' side of the bar eating a meal, as was the third, except that he was behind the counter.

Moving on, the little Oriental reached the front end of the *cantina*. However, he halted in the alley and listened for Ole Devil. Once again, the rain proved to be beneficial. The normally hard surface of the street was sufficiently softened for the horses to approach with little or no noise.

Holding the animals to a walk, Ole Devil was scanning the buildings on each side of the street. He had noticed that the lookout was no longer outside the *cantina* and wondered whether that was because the man whom they were expecting had arrived, or if he was now keeping watch from a less exposed position.

'Two have left, Devil-san!' Tommy hissed as his companion rode by.

'*Bueno!*' the Texian answered, in no louder tones, without halting until he had turned the horses to face the hitching rail near the cantina's door.

Shortly after the party had broken into the *cantina* their leader, Sid Halford had ordered Joe Stiple to search the building for liquor to supplement their meagre supply. Although Stiple had failed to do so, he had stayed behind the bar. Having been a bartender, he always felt more at home on the sober side of the counter. Standing there, he was the first to become aware of Ole Devil's arrival.

'Hey!' Stiple ejaculated. 'Somebody's just rid by the window.'

'It could be Soapy and Al coming back,' suggested the lanky man who had acted as lookout, speaking through a mouth filled with pemmican.

'I don't reckon so,' Stiple objected. 'Looked like there was only one man and he's come from the east.'

While the brief conversation had been going on, Halford, the lookout — whose name was Mucker — and the *vaquero* Arnaldo

69

Verde, had turned towards the door. They heard the horses being brought to a halt and leather creaking as the rider dismounted, but as yet they could not see him. Halford and Mucker reached towards their rifles. Behind the bar, Stiple was duplicating Verde's actions by placing his right hand on the butt of the pistol that was thrust through his belt.

'Easy there, gents,' called the newcomer, as he crossed the sidewalk. 'I saw the light and came in to see if I could stay here for the night.'

Studying the tall, whipcord slender young man, and giving first attention to the way he was dressed and armed, Verde then examined his features. He was reminded of pictures he had seen of the Devil.

Juglares had said that the man being sent by Houston to collect the rifles had a face like *el Diablo*, the Devil!

On receiving the *major domo's* information, Verde had known that he would need help to deal with it. The nearest available assistance had been a group of white renegades who were working for the Mexicans. Going to their camp, he had told their leader what he had learned. It had been decided that Halford's party would accompany Verde and kill Houston's officer. Once that had been done, the band would go to the coast and capture the shipment.

Guessing that their victim – who, according to Juglares, would be travelling alone – was almost certain to make use of the trail between San Antonio and Gonzales, the party had sought for him along it. Finding the hamlet deserted shortly after the rain had started to fall, they had forced an entry into the *cantina*. Discussing the matter, Verde and Halford had concluded that the man they were seeking would also use it for shelter when he arrived.

The gamble had only partially paid off!

In some way, the Texian had eluded Al and Soapy who had left in the hope of locating him. However, he was strolling into the *cantina* and clearly had no suspicion of the fate that awaited him.

For all that, Verde realized things could go wrong. Finding himself confronted by four men, all of whom were fingering weapons, the newcomer had halted just inside the door. If any of the party attempted to raise a pistol or rifle, he would leap back out of the building. Before the swiftest of them could reach the sidewalk, he would be mounted and riding away.

70

It was a moment for rapid thought!

Having done so, Verde put his scheme into operation and silently prayed that his companions would guess what he was doing and respond correctly.

'Hey, *amigos*, it's all right,' Verde announced in a hearty tone, taking his hand away from the pistol. 'I know this man. It's *Captain Hardin* of the Texas Light Cavalry. *Saludos* captain. It's good to see you.'

With that, the *vaquero* started to walk forward. His manner was friendly and he held out his right hand. In a sheath strapped to the inside of his left forearm, hidden from sight by his jacket's sleeve yet ready to slip into his grasp when necessary, was a needle-pointed, razor-sharp knife. He was an expert at producing and using it unexpectedly.

CHAPTER SEVEN

THEY WERE WAITING FOR *YOU*

OLE DEVIL HARDIN watched the *vaquero* coming towards him, but also devoted some of his attention to the three white men. That they should have reached for their weapons on his arrival neither surprised nor alarmed him. It was a simple precaution that anybody would be expected to take in such troubled times. However, he had noticed how the lanky former lookout had thrown a startled glance at the biggest of the party on hearing his name. What was more, despite the *vaquero's* apparent friendliness and his announcement of Ole Devil's identity, the trio were showing little sign of relaxing.

Watching Verde advancing, Halford suddenly realized what the welcome meant. He turned his head just in time to see Mucker, who was not the most intelligent of the party, starting to lift his flintlock. Taking his own right hand from his rifle, Halford gave the lanky man a swift jab on the arm. On Mucker swinging a puzzled gaze at him, he scowled prohibitively and shook his head. Looking back at Verde and the Texian, Halford replaced his hand on his own rifle. He did not notice that, although refraining from lifting the weapon, Mucker did not move his hand away.

At first, Ole Devil had decided that the white men might have an antipathy towards officers. However, having observed the by-play between Halford and Mucker, he felt decidedly uneasy. His instincts suggested that everything might not be so amiable as the *vaquero* was making out.

Showing nothing of his suspicions, Ole Devil stepped forward. He did not recognize the *vaquero*, but knew that meant little. Without growing boastful about it, he knew that he had already carved something of a name for himself since arriving in Texas. What was more, his appearance was so distinctive — particularly since, as a joke more than anything, he had grown the moustache and beard to augment his Mephistophelian features – that he attracted attention and remembrance. Possibily the *vaquero* had seen him somewhere and was wanting to impress the three white men by a pretence of a much closer acquaintanceship than was the case.

Despite the conclusions which he had drawn, Ole Devil could not throw off his sense of perturbation. Something, he felt sure, was wrong. The burly hard-case had stopped the former lookout from lifting the flintlock, but had returned his own hand to his rifle. The third man's hands were hidden by the counter and might already be grasping a firearm.

However, the *vaquero* continued to draw nearer. He was still smiling, with his right hand extended to be shaken and the left hanging by his side. Neither were anywhere near the heavy pistol which was thrust, butt forward, through the silk sash around his waist and he had no other visible weapon.

Although Ole Devil was not yet within reaching distance of the *vaquero*, he too thrust out his right hand. He realized that he might be doing the occupants of the bar-room an injustice by mistrusting them. They would find such an attitude offensive if they were innocent of evil intent. Being aware of the kind of pride and temper possessed by many Texians, he was alert to the possibility that they might try to avenge what they would regard as an insult to their integrity and he wanted to avoid trouble of that nature. Also, to continue delaying a response to the *vaquero's* friendly greeting was almost sure to arouse their suspicions if his own feelings should be justified.

'*Saludos, senor,*' the young Texian said, but he did not relax his vigilance and was ready to react with all the speed if the *vaquero* should try to draw a weapon. He took the opportunity to study the men at the bar, continuing, 'Howdy, gents.'

Elated by the success of his scheme to lull the newcomer into a sense of false security, Verde gave the special twist to his left arm that liberated the knife from its sheath. Without needing to look, he caught the hilt as it slid into his hand, which was turned with the knuckles forward to prevent his potential victim from seeing what was happening. Easing back the hand so that it was concealed by his thigh, he turned the weapon deftly until its blade was extended ahead of his thumb and forefinger.

All was now ready for an upwards thrust into the unsuspecting Texian's stomach!

The blow would be delivered as soon as they were shaking

hands, so that the victim could not step back and avoid it.

At the bar, Mucker started to grin broadly as he watched the knife appear in Verde's left hand. He darted a delighted glance at Halford, but it was not returned. Equally aware of what was going on, the big man began to lift his rifle with the right hand so he would be ready in case something went wrong and Verde failed to do his work.

One more stride would bring Ole Devil and the *vaquero* close enough to shake hands. While the other's features still retained their friendly aspect, the Texian noticed that his left hand had, apparently by accident, swung until it was out of sight. Glancing past the *vaquero*, Ole Devil observed the expression of triumph on Mucker's face, and the movements of Halford. He sensed that the situation might be far less innocuous than appeared on the surface.

Suddenly the young Texian felt as if a cold hand had pressed against his spine.

The *vaquero* was armed with a pistol, but did not appear to be wearing a knife!

Ole Devil realized that not every member of the Spanish or Mexican races had a natural affinity towards knife-fighting, but it was extremely rare to come across a *vaquero* who did not go armed with one. If it was not sheathed on his belt, or thrust through his sash, it might be suspended beneath his collar at the back of the neck, carried in the top of his boot, or hidden in some other way.

There was one place of concealment, Ole Devil remembered having been told, which assassins in many lands made use of.

Reaching to take hold of the young Texian's hand and confident that he suspected nothing, Verde tensed slightly and was ready to bring out the knife. Before he could do so, he felt his intended victim's fingers make contact.

But not with his hand!

Hoping that his motives would be understood and his apologies accepted if he was mistaken, Ole Devil acted with deadly speed. Instead of allowing his hand to be trapped, he changed its direction slightly. Without giving any indication of his intentions, he grasped the *vaquero's* right wrist tightly. As he did so, he took a step to the right and rear and swung so that, for a moment, he was standing at an angle away from Verde. Before the *vaquero* could resist, he jerked on the wrist with all his strength and pivoted himself around on his right foot. Bending his other leg, he swung it in a circular motion which propelled the knee into the advancing man's stomach.

Taken unawares, Verde could not prevent himself from being dragged forward. The knee met his midsection with considerable force. With his wrist released at the moment of impact, he was driven backwards. His knife slipped from his fingers and clattered to the floor as, partially winded and starting to fold over, he twisted away from his assailant. It was an almost instinctive action, designed to shield him from any further attack by the Texian, and he stumbled against the table at which he and his companions had been seated.

'Get the bastard!' Halford roared, snatching up his rifle in the expectation that their potential victim would turn and run.

Seeing Verde's assassination attempt fail, Stiple started to respond without needing the burly man's advice. What was more, he was in a better position to do something than either of his companions. Knowing that he could do so without being seen by the Texian, he had already drawn the pistol from his belt. Jerking back the hammer, he started to raise the weapon above the level of the bar which had previously hidden his movements.

Although startled by the unexpected turn of events, Mucker made a grab for his long rifle.

Instead of justifying the burly man's expectation and running, Ole Devil set his weight on his spread apart feet. Bending his knees slightly and inclining his torso forward a little, he made preparations for fighting back.

While prudence might have dictated that the young Texian should adopt the course Halford was anticipating, he had no intention of running. Hot-tempered arrogance had nothing to do with the decision. The fact that the *vaquero* had identified him in such a manner aroused disturbing possibilities which he considered must be investigated. Nor was his decision to seek a solution made rashly. He had devoted a lot of time, thought and effort to developing the means of defending himself in such a situation.

Even before coming to Texas, Ole Devil had realized that there were several flaws in the training which he had received in handling a pistol. His instructors had regarded a handgun as a duelling implement, with rules and conventions limiting how it could be used, rather than as a readily accessible defensive weapon. With the latter purpose in mind, he had worked out a technique that was very effective.

Turning palm outwards, Ole Devil's right hand flashed to and closed around the butt of the Manton pistol. To slide the weapon free from the belt's retaining loop, he used a system which would eventually be developed into the 'high cavalry-twist' draw.* However, unlike the gun fighters who perfected the method in the mid-1860's and later, his sequence of firing could not be carried out with just one hand. Instead because of the shape and position of the hammer, he had to use the heel of his left palm almost as if he was 'fanning' the hammer of a single action revolver.

The unorthodox method of handling the pistol did not end with the way it had been twisted free from the belt and turned towards its target. Instead of adopting the accepted stance – sideways, with the right hand fully extended at shoulder height, left arm bent and hand on the hip – of the formal duellist, he stood squarely to his point of aim. Crouching slightly, he elevated the weapon to eye-level and, after cocking the hammer, his left hand went around to cup under the support the right. While doing so, he was selecting the man who was posing the most immediate threat to his life.

Not for another thirty or so years would the idea of fast drawing and shooting become widely known, or practised. So Ole Devil's actions came as a surprise and a shock to the three men at the bar, particularly to Stiple. With his pistol lifting to the firing position, he found himself looking into the unwavering muzzle of the Texian's weapon. The hole of the barrel seemed to be much larger than its usual .54 of an inch calibre.

Having made sure of his aim, Ole Devil squeezed the trigger. On the hammer driving forward, the superiority of the caplock system became apparent. Striking directly on to the brass percussion cap, without the need to push clear the frizzen and create sparks, it was much faster in operation. Flame and white smoke gushed out of the muzzle about two seconds after his hand had closed around the butt.

Ole Devil fired the only way he dared under the circumstances. Flying across the room, the soft lead ball went by Hal-

* A more detailed description of the 'high cavalry twist' draw is given in: *Slip Gun.*

ford as he was swinging his rifle towards his shoulder and struck Stiple in the centre of the forehead. It ranged onwards, to burst out at the rear of the skull accompanied by a spray of blood, brains and shattered fragments of bone. Killed instantly, the stricken man was flung backwards. The pistol dropped from his nerveless hand as he crashed into the wall. Then he crumpled as if he had been boned and fell out of sight behind the counter.

Although somewhat perturbed by the young Texian's spirited and very effective resistance in the face of danger, Halford still continued to raise the rifle. He drew consolation from the realization that, no matter how fast and capable a shot the other might be, the pistol was now empty. Long before Hardin could reload, or try to protect himself in some other fashion, Halford would have drawn a bead on him and sent a bullet into the head.

Even as the thought came to the burly man, he discovered that – in spite of the information which Verde had given on the subject – their intended victim was not travelling alone or unescorted.

Having moved silently down the sidewalk, bending low as he went by the window, Tommy Okasi was standing alongside the door by the time that Ole Devil had passed through. The little Oriental had not shown himself until he had heard the commotion which had warned him that his intervention might be necessary.

Darting across the threshold and into the bar-room, Tommy studied the situation with the eye of a tactician. One glance told him which of the remaining enemies was posing the most immediate threat to his companion. The *vaquero* was sprawled face down across the table. At the bar, showing his bewilderment, Mucker was making a belated grab for his rifle. Neither, Tommy realized, was so dangerous as the burly man. His weapon would soon be lined and able to open fire. At such a short range, he was not likely to miss.

Coming to a halt with his feet spread to an angle of roughly sixty degrees, Tommy turned the upper part of his body to the left and looked at his target. In a smoothly flowing, but very fast move, the long bow rose until perpendicular and was lifted until his hands were higher than his head. Extending his left arm until it was straight and shoulder high, he drew the string back and down with his right hand until the flight of the arrow was almost brushing against his off ear.* By the time his draw was completed, he was sighting so that two imaginary lines — one extended from his right eye and the other out of the arrow — intersected on Halford's left breast. Satisfied, he released his hold on the string.

Liberated from its tension, the bow's limbs returned to their previous positions. In doing so, they propelled the arrow forward. Hissing viciously through the air, the shaft flew towards its mark. On arriving, the needle-pointed, razor sharp, horizontal head cut between the ribs. It sliced open the heart in passing, to emerge through his back and sank into the bar.

Involuntarily throwing aside his unfired rifle as a spasm of agony ripped through him, Halford wrenched the arrow from the counter. Then he spun around with his hands clawing ineffectually at the shaft which was protruding from his chest and crashed dying to the floor.

With his left fingers closing around the barrel of the rifle so that he could elevate it into the firing position, Mucker saw first Stiple and then Halford struck down. He continued to lift the weapon instinctively, turning a worried gaze on the men who were responsible for his companions' deaths. What he discovered was not calculated to reduce his anxiety. The young Texian was starting to move forward, transferring the still smoking pistol to his left hand so that the right could go across to the ivory hilt of the bowie knife. Beyond him, the small 'Chinaman' was already reaching for another arrow.

Lying across the table which had prevented him from falling to the floor, Verde was also studying Ole Devil and Tommy. While a capable knife-fighter and no coward, the *vaquero* had more sense than to tangle with the Texian in his present condition. Not only had he lost his knife, but he also lacked the other's ability to draw and fire a pistol swiftly, and he was still feeling the effects of the knee kick. What was more, contrary to Juglares's information, their would-be victim was not alone. Nor was he likely to have restricted his escort to one small man armed with such primitive, if effective, weapons. In all probability, the rest of the escort were approaching ready to support the advance pair.

While these thoughts were passing through Verde's head, fright was spurring Mucker to move at speed. Already the butt

* A description of Occidental archery techniques is given in: *Bunduki.*

78

of the rifle was cradled against his shoulder and its barrel was pointing at the centre of the Texian's chest. His right hand drew back the hammer, then returned to enfold the wrist of the butt and his forefinger entered the triggerguard.

Deciding that discretion was by far the better part of valour under the circumstances, Verde lurched erect. Moving around, he hooked his hands under the edge of the table and flung it in Ole Devil's direction. Precipitated to the floor, the lamp – which the party had found behind the bar on their arrival – was shattered. It was almost out of fuel, so did not burst into flames. Instead, it went out and, as the moon had disappeared behind some clouds, the room was plunged into darkness.

Holding the pistol in his left hand and with the right engaged in drawing the bowie knife, Ole Devil could do nothing more than leap aside as the table was thrown his way. However, the evasion saved his life. Mucker's rifle roared an instant before the lamp was extinguished and its bullet passed where Ole Devil's torso had been a moment earlier.

Turning as soon as the darkness had descended, Verde ran across the room. He was making for where an oblong, slightly lighter than the surrounding blackness, marked the window in the left wall.

Realizing that he had missed the Texian and hearing his companion's footsteps, Mucker did not hesitate. He had no intention of testing his strength against such an efficient fighter as their victim had proved to be, especially as Verde clearly had no intention of staying. Having reached his decision, the lanky man flung his rifle towards where he had last seen the Texian so that it revolved parallel to the floor.

Luck was on Mucker's side.

Starting to follow the *vaquero* with the intention of intercepting and capturing him, Ole Devil felt the barrel of the rifle passing between his legs. He was tripped, pitching forward through the blackness. Instinctively he let go of the pistol and the knife, so that he would have a better chance of breaking his fall.

There was a shattering crash of breaking glass and timber. Covering his face with his forearms, Verde had hurled himself through the window. Carrying the ruined frame and broken panes with him, he plunged into the alley. Landing on his feet, he darted towards the lean-to.

At the door, Tommy had started to draw the bow and was

79

watching the window as he had guessed that the *vaquero* would attempt to leave through it. When the sound of Ol Devil falling reached his ears, he could not prevent himself from looking in that direction. The commotion caused by Verde's departure brought the little Oriental's attention back to the window. He realized that he was too late to stop the *vaquero*. Nor was he any too sanguine over his chances of being able to do anything about the lanky white man, who he felt sure would follow the *vaquero*. Accurate aiming in the almost pitch blackness of the room was far from easy. In fact, Tommy could not even be sure of exactly where his arrow was pointing.

Listening to Mucker as he sprinted across the room, Tommy waited with the bow fully drawn. When he saw the other's vague silhouette, he loosed the shaft. It flew high, but came very close to scoring a hit. Mucker felt the hat snatched from his head as if by an invisible hand and heard the thud as the arrow which had impaled it drove into the ruined frame of the window. The sensation gave him an added incentive to leave. Letting out a screech, he flung himself recklessly through the hole. Although he came down on his hands and knees, he was up like a flash and racing after his companion.

'Are you all right, Devil-san?' Tommy called anxiously, lowering the bow.

'Sure,' the Texian answered, feeling along the floor for his bowie knife. 'See if you can stop them!'

Satisfied that his companion was not hurt, Tommy turned and went out of the door. He found the linebacked dun and the bay were moving restlessly, but not so badly frightened by the commotion that they were threatening to pull free the reins and bolt. So taking another arrow from the quiver, he nocked it to the bow's string and trotted along the sidewalk.

Even before Tommy reached the alley, he could hear enough to warn him that he might not be able to carry out his companion's order. The moon was still behind the clouds, which had reduced the visibility. While he could not see that far, the sounds suggested the two men were already leading their mounts from the lean-to. Leather creaked as they swung into their saddles, then the animals started moving.

Tommy increased his pace, but by the time he arrived at the rear of the *cantina* the men were galloping to the west. Although he brought the bow into the shooting position, he did not bother to draw back on the string. Having only twenty arrows, he did not want to chance losing one while trying to hit a practically impossible target. Waiting until he was sure that the pair did not intend to return, he replaced the arrow and walked through the alley. On reaching the street, he found Ole Devil was standing on the sidewalk.

'Any luck?' the Texian inquired, sheathing his knife.

'They were gone before I could shoot,' Tommy replied. 'Who were they?'

'I don't know,' Ole Devil admitted. 'It's a pity we couldn't have taken at least one of them alive and questioned him. I've an idea they weren't here by accident, or just to shelter from the rain.'

'You mean that they were waiting for *you*? Tommy asked.

'I started to think so,' Ole Devil answered. 'But this isn't the shortest way from San Antonio to Santa Cristobal Bay. So, even if they'd learned about the shipment in some way, they wouldn't have expected to find me on this trail.'

'Unless they knew how you are going to carry the rifles,' Tommy supplemented.

'How could they?' Ole Devil demanded. 'Only General Sam and I knew that.'

'I heard the first two that left talking as they went,' Tommy explained. 'One was saying something about the town being out of the man they were expecting's way and the other said they'd been told he was going to Gonzales first.'

'Then it could have been *me* they were after,' Ole Devil breathed, remembering the conclusions he had drawn from the men's behaviour when he had arrived.

What was more, the young Texian saw the implications if his assumption was correct. Somebody very close to General Houston must be a traitor and was supplying information to the Mexicans. He also realized that there would not be time to return and warn the General, then reach the rendezvous with the ship. Before he could do so, it would have been forced to depart and the consignment of rifles would be lost to Texas.

CHAPTER EIGHT

IF YOU CAN'T HELP ME,
DON'T HELP THE BEAR!

DESPITE the fact that he arrived at Gonzales without any further difficulties or attempts upon his life, Ole Devil Hardin refused to let himself be lulled into what he suspected might be a sense of false security. Even the fact that he was now riding across the range between the town and Ewart Brindley's property did not cause him to relax his vigilance. Rather the knowledge tended to increase it.

Having taken precautions in case the *vaquero* and Mucker should return with the two men who had departed earlier, Ole Devil and Tommy Okasi had made their preparations to spend the night at the hamlet. After attending to their horses and those of the dead men, they had made a meal from the rations of jerked beef and pemmican which they were carrying. Then they had resumed their investigations into the ramifications of the incident at the *cantina*.

A thorough search of the two bodies had produced one very significant piece of evidence. In a concealed pocket at the back of the larger corpse's belt there had been a document bearing the Mexican coat-of-arms and a message written in Spanish. It was to inform all members of Santa Anna's forces that the bearer, Sidney Halford, was working for the Mexican Government and must be given any assistance that he requested. Although his companion had not been in possession of a similar authorization, it was convincing proof that they were not loyal to the Republic of Texas.

Unfortunately, there had been nothing to suggest why the renegades were at the hamlet.

Being aware of the very serious issues involved, Ole Devil and Tommy had discussed the matter at great length and in detail.

First they had considered the way in which the *vaquero* had acted when Ole Devil had entered the *cantina*. If the gang had merely been awaiting the arrival of a companion, there was no reason for him to have behaved in such a manner. He might, of course, have been alerting the other members of the party to the fact that the newcomer was rather more important than a chance-passing member of the Republic of Texas's army. However, the lanky man's reaction to the introduction had implied that he, for one, wanted to discover who had arrived.

Against that, the gang had apparently expected only one man. If they had known who was being sent to collect the rifles, they must have acquired their knowledge from what had been said in General Samuel Houston's office. Which meant that somebody had been able to listen to the conversation without the General and Ole Devil being aware of it. However, if that had been the case, the eavesdropper would have known that Tommy was accompanying the young Texian. Unless, as the little Oriental had pointed out, for some reason he – or she – had been prevented from hearing all that had passed between them.

There was, Ole Devil had realized, only one course open to him. If there should be a spy with the means of gathering such confidential information, the General must be warned so that he could take precautions. Producing a writing-case from his war bag, the young Texian had composed a report for Houston. In it, he had given a comprehensive description of the incident and of the conclusions which he and Tommy had reached. He had also said that he was retaining the document which identified Halford in case he might find a need for it during the assignment.

The next morning, after having spent an otherwise uneventful night in the *cantina*, Ole Devil had sent Tommy back to San Antonio de Bexar with the report. Using one of the dead men's horses, which the fleeing pair had been in too much of a hurry either to take with them or frighten away, the little Oriental was to ride relay. After delivering the information to Houston, he would follow and rejoin Ole Devil on the way to the rendezvous at Santa Cristobal Bay.

Taking along the second of the horses which had been left in the lean-to – the contents of the bed roll on the cantle of its 'slick fork' saddle, although supplying no information of greater use, suggested that it had been Halford's property – Ole

Devil had resumed his journey at dawn, Tommy was using Stiple's mount, which had a Walker-style rig, having lost the toss of a coin to determine which of them should take it.

Once again the young Texian had not stuck to the trail. While the two men had fled and not returned, he doubted whether they and their companions would give up so easily; especially if they were aware of his assignment and were trying to prevent him from carrying it out. He had reached Guadalupe without having seen any sign of them. Visiting the town, he had found its population were preparing to take part in the withdrawal to the east.

The commanding officer of the town's small garrison had listened to Ole Devil's story and, without having asked too many questions about the nature of his mission, had promised to send a patrol to the hamlet. They were to search along the trail on the very slender chance that the four men might still be lurking in the vicinity. Although Ole Devil had described the quartet as well as possible and the officer had said that he would try to find out if they had been seen around Guadalupe, he doubted if he would be successful as there were so many strangers present. However, he had offered to supply Ole Devil with an escort as far as Gonzales. Wanting to travel faster than would be possible if he was accompanied by a number of men, as well as having no wish to reduce the other's already barely adequate force, the young Texian had declined the offer and had ridden on alone.

As was always his way, Ole Devil had given much thought to the situation. While he had remained alert and watchful, he had not expected to run into any trouble before he had passed through Gonzales on the final five or so miles which separated it from the Brindleys' place. His reasoning was that if the men were hunting him because of the shipment, and had been told of at least part of the arrangements he had made in Houston's office, they would know why he was not taking the most direct route to Santa Cristobal Bay. After the way in which he had arrived at the hamlet, they were likely to assume that he would adopt similar tactics and stay off the trail. While there were a number of ways in which he could travel from Guadalupe to Gonzales, once he had passed the latter town his route would be more restricted.

In view of his conclusions, Ole Devil was willing to bet that they would be spread out and keeping watch for him somewhere between two and four miles beyond Gonzales. Nearer to the town, or closer to the Brindleys' ranch, any shooting would be heard and might – almost certainly would if there was more than one shot – be investigated. Now he had already entered the region where, if his assumptions were correct, he could expect to find them.

Slouching comfortably in the saddle of the borrowed horse, with the linebacked bay walking at its right side, the young Texian kept his eyes constantly on the move. He was passing through rolling, broken and bush-dotted terrain which would offer plenty of scope for ambush. What was more, there were numerous areas of high ground; vantage points from which the quartet could keep watch for him. However, it was also the kind of land that allowed a man to move without making himself too conspicuous if he knew how to utilize it and did not mind winding about instead of trying to go directly to his ultimate destination.

Since his arrival in Texas, Ole Devil had learned how to make the most use of such land when he was traversing it. Despite his upbringing, in fact because of it, he was no snob. Nor had he ever been so self-opinionated that he would not take advice and learn from those who knew what they were talking about. Working with experienced frontier men, he had watched, listened, remembered and put his findings into practice. He was doing so now as he rode along, leading the dun with its reins held in his left hand.

Having called at Gonzales and obtained advice on how to find the Brindleys' ranch, Ole Devil had kept to the bottom of draws, or passed through areas of bushes instead of going across more easily negotiable open ground. When he had been compelled to expose himself by crossing a ridge, he had done so with great care and only after scanning every inch of the land ahead and behind.

The raucous cackle of feeding magpies came to Ole Devil's ears as he was approaching the top of a bush-fringed rim. Suddenly, one of the black and white scavengers gave an alarm call and they rose into the air. The young Texian realized that it was not his presence which had frightened them.

Slowing down his horses, Ole Devil approached the rim with extreme care. Making use of the screen of bushes, he peered over the top. About a hundred yards away, a buckskin-clad figure carrying a rifle was walking towards the partially eaten carcass of a mule that lay in the open some thirty yards from a clump of buffalo-berry bushes.

Although the figure was dressed in a familiar manner, except that he had on Indian moccasins and leggings instead of boots, and despite the brim of the hat hiding his face as he looked down at the carcass, Ole Devil knew he was not one of the white men who had been in the *cantina*. About five foot seven inches tall, while neither puny nor skinny, he lacked the thickset bulk of the one who compared with him in height. In addition, he gave the impression of being younger. His horse, a black and white *tobiano* gelding with a 'slick fork' saddle that had a coiled rope strapped to its horn, but no bed roll on the cantle, was standing ground-hitched some thirty feet away. It was staring in alarmed manner at the dead mule.

The horse, Ole Devil decided, was showing better sense than its owner.

Even as the thought came, there was a rustling among the buffalo-berry bushes. Ole Devil looked that way and a sense of chilly apprehension drove through him. From all appearances, the youngster's desire to examine the dead mule had led him into a potentially dangerous situation. Rearing up on its hind legs, a large bear loomed over the bushes. It had been lying up in the shade after feeding on the carcass, Snorting and snuffling, it stared at the intruder advancing towards its kill.

For a moment, Ole Devil was alarmed on the youngster's behalf. Then, with a feeling of relief, he realized that the bear – despite its size – was of the black species and not, as he had first feared, a grizzly. Despite the many highly-spiced, horrifying stories told about its savage nature, *Euarctos Americanus*, the American black bear, was generally not especially dangerous to human beings. If the creature in the bushes had been a Texas flat-headed grizzly, the youngster's position would have been very precarious. Fortunately for him, that part of Texas was somewhat to the east of *Ursus Texensis Texensis*'s range.

With the realization, Ole Devil felt the apprehension leaving him. He had no wish to advertise his presence and attract unwanted attention by shooting. All the black bears he had come into contact with had never lingered any longer than necessary in the presence of human beings, even when disturbed after having fed on a kill. It was merely curious and puzzled. Being short-sighted like all of its species, it was not sure what kind of creature was standing near its prey. However, as long as the youngster did nothing to antagonize it, there was a better than fair chance that he could withdraw in safety.

'You mule-killing son-of-a-bitch!'

Even as Ole Devil opened his mouth to call and advise the youngster to back away slowly, the boy yelled at the bear and started to raise his rifle. Excitement, or fear, had given his voice a high pitched, almost feminine sounding timbre.

Hearing the youngster, the bear showed that it might be different in habits from most others of its species. Instead of giving a 'whoof!' of alarm on hearing the human voice, spinning around and taking off for a safer location at all speed, it cut loose with a short, rasping and menacing, coughing noise.

Ole Devil had only once before heard a similar sound, but he had never forgotten that occasion. It had happened during a hunt in Louisiana and the bear had given just such a cough before charging through the pack of hounds to try and reach the hunters. Several bullets had been required to put the enraged beast down.

Instead of taking warning from the bear's behaviour, the youngster stood his ground. Lining the rifle, which he must have cocked as he was approaching the carcass, he squeezed the trigger. The hammer fell. There was a puff of smoke from the frizzen pan, but the main charge failed to ignite for some reason.

As if realizing what the hissing splutter from the rifle meant, the bear gave another of its threatening coughs and lurched forward.

To give the youngster credit, he might have acted in an impulsive and reckless manner by yelling and trying to shoot the bear, but he was no fool. Nor, despite how his voice had sounded, did he panic. As the bear dropped on to all fours and burst from the fringe of the buffalo-berry bushes, he let his useless rifle fall and turned. However, having already been disturbed and made nervous by the bloody carcass, or perhaps because it had caught the bear's scent, the *tobiano* gelding did not wait for its master to return and mount. At the sight of the rage-bristling beast erupting into view, the horse gave a squeal of terror and, disregarding the dangling split-ended reins, bolted.

Growling a curse, Ole Devil used his spurs to set the borrowed horse into motion. Feeling the tug at its reins, the dun advanced and kept pace with its companion as they topped the ridge. However, as much as he would liked to have done, the young Texian knew he could not delay or slow down and transfer to his own mount.

Once again, the youngster was displaying courage. Certainly he had sufficient good sense to keep running. He had a lead over the bear which might just about prove adequate providing that he could maintain or increase his pace. Unfortunately, he was going away from Ole Devil. To call on him to change direction would be fatal. So the young Texian kept quiet and urged his mount to a gallop. Then he discarded the dun's reins to leave both his hands free.

A black bear could attain a speed of around twenty-five miles an hour when charging, but it needed time to build up to its top pace. With its eyes fixed on the fleeing youngster, it hurtled after him and ignored the departing horse. Nor was it aware of Ole Devil dashing down the slope in its direction.

Urging the borrowed horse to its fastest gait, the young Texian gave thought to how he might best deal with the situation. He had heard that some Indian braves had so little fear of the black bear that they regarded it as being unworthy of death by arrow, lance, tomahawk, firearm, or even a knife. Instead, the warrior would beat the beast's brains out with a club and apologize to its spirit for having done so. However, having done a fair amount of bear hunting, Ole Devil had never believed the story. He certainly was not inclined to try and duplicate the feat, particularly under the prevailing conditions.

Nor, despite the fact that the Browning rifle when loaded – which it was not at that moment due to the difficulty of carrying it in a condition of readiness – would have offered him the advantage of five consecutive shots without needing recharging, did he regret that it was in the dun's saddleboot. To have drawn it and made it ready for firing would be a very difficult, if not impossible, task when riding at full speed. What was more, from his present position, all he could take aim at was the bear's rump. A hit there with the comparatively small calibre rifle would not stop it quickly enough to save the youngster from a mauling. Ole Devil would have to place a bullet in exactly the right spot to achieve his purpose. Luckily, due to having transferred his weapon carrier to the borrowed horse's saddlehorn, he would have two shots at his disposal instead of only one. For all that, killing the bear would be far from a sinecure.

When in motion at speed, a black bear's rolling, loose-haired hide and the placement of its feet combine to present ever-changing contours which made accurate aiming a difficult proposition. Throughout its stride, its legs 'scissored' rapidly to add to the confusion. One moment the forepaws would be under the rump and the back legs up close to the nose, bunching the vital organs. Next the body appeared to become extended out of all proportion, causing the target to change its position in relation to the now elongated frame. The young Texian knew of only one area where he could rely upon hitting and bringing down the animal immediately.

There was, however, a major objection to Ole Devil firing even a single shot. It might be heard by the *vaquero* and his companions, causing them to come and investigate.

For a moment, Ole Devil contemplated trying to effect a rescue in the manner of a Comanche brave going to a wounded or unhorsed companion's assistance. He had practised the method with other members of Company 'C' and was proficient at it. Doing so under the prevailing conditions would be difficult and dangerous, yet it might be possible if the youngster co-operated. The problem was how to acquaint him with what was being planned. Calling out the information was not the answer. It was sure to distract him and would cause him to slow down, or could even make him stumble if he looked back to see who had spoken.

Then another factor arose to lessen the already slender hope of scooping up the youngster and carrying him to safety. A worried snort burst from the fast-moving horse as its flaring nostrils picked up the bear's scent. Controlling its desire to shy away from a natural enemy, Ole Devil managed to keep it running in a straight line. Clearly the borrowed mount lacked the stability of temperament for him to risk that kind of a rescue. An unexpected swerve, a refusal to respond to his heels' signals – his hands would be fully occupied with the pick up and could not manipulate the reins – or a panic-induced stumble might see them all on the ground and tangled with the enraged bear.

While a black bear could not equal the grizzly's armament, its teeth and claws were sufficiently well-developed for Ole Devil to have the greatest reluctance to feel them sink into his flesh.

Discarding the idea of making a Comanche-style rescue, Ole Devil drew the Manton pistol – mate to the one in his belt loop

— from the holster on his weapon-carrier and cocked its hammer. Already he was alongside the bear and the horse's speed was carrying them by. No sooner had they drawn ahead than he saw the youngster trip and go sprawling.

There was no time to lose!

Tossing his left leg forward and over the saddlehorn, the young Texian quit the horse at full gallop. He landed with an almost cat-like agility which told of long and arduous training. His momentum carried him onwards a few strides, until he had almost reached the youngster who had managed to break his fall and was attempting to rise. Coming to a stop, Ole Devil swung around and brought the pistol up to arm's length and eye level. Once again, he adopted the double handed grip on the butt that had served him so well in the *cantina*.

Rushing closer, the bear made an awe-inspiring sight. Its coat was bristling with rage until it seemed far larger than its already not inconsiderable size. Uttering savage, blood-chilling snarls, its open, slavering jaws were filled with long and sharp teeth. Its slightly curved, almost needle-pointed claws, tore grooves in the ground and sent dirt flying as they helped to propel it towards its intended prey. All in all, the furious three hundred pound beast was not a spectacle to inspire confidence, or even peace of mind, when one was facing it armed with nothing more than a pistol which held only a single shot and could not be re-loaded quickly.

'Lord!' Ole Devil breathed, in an attempt to control his rising tension as he looked along the nine inch, octagonal barrel at the approaching animal. 'If you can't help me, don't help the bear!'

While the young Texian found himself repeating the line from the old Negro comic song, 'The Preacher And The Bear', he was also aligning the 'V' notch of the rear- and blade of the front-sights on the centre of the approaching animal's head. An area the size of the top of the bear's skull would have been comparatively easy to hit at such close range, on a stationary paper target. However, even to a man of Ole Devil's skill, it seemed much smaller and vastly more difficult at that moment. He knew that he would have time for only the one shot. So it had to strike accurately or somebody, himself for sure and in all probability the youngster he was attempting to save, was going to be killed.

Forcing himself to remain calm and to wait until certain of

his aim, Ole Devil made allowance for the bear's forward movement and squeezed the trigger. Forty grains of powder were waiting to be ignited and turned into a mass of gas which would thrust the half-ounce ball through the barrel's rifling grooves. It was a very heavy charge and would be capable of inflicting considerable damage – providing a hit was made.

On the other hand, if the pistol should hang fire for some reason – as the youngster's rifle had – Ole Devil would be unlikely to survive. Even if he did, he would be too badly injured to carry on with his assignment.

CHAPTER NINE

HE'LL SKIN YOU ALIVE!

NEVER had the hammer of the Manton pistol seemed to be moving so slowly!

It fell, at long last, striking the brass percussion cap!

Still moving to compensate for the bear's ever changing – and nearing – position, the pistol roared!

Converging with the approaching beast, the .54 calibre bullet struck it between and slightly above the eyes to plough through into the brain. Hit while its forelegs were approaching the end of a rearwards thrust, the bear began to crumple forward.

Even as smoke partially obscured the bear and the pistol's barrel rose under the impulsion of the recoil, without waiting to discover the effect of the shot, Old Devil Hardin sprang to his right. Dropping the empty weapon, he sent his right hand curling back and around the butt of the pistol's mate. Twisting it free from the retainer loop on his belt, he was just starting to draw back the hammer with the heel of his left palm when the bear emerged from the smoke. However, it was turning a somersault and it crashed to the ground on its back. With its jaws chomping in a hideous fashion and legs flailing their death throes, it slid to a halt on the very spot Hardin had just vacated.

It was, the young Texian decided, as narrow an escape from a painful death as had ever come his way.

Suddenly, courageous as he was, Ole Devil found that he was perspiring very freely and breathing as heavily as if he had run a mile. What was more, his limbs were shaking from the reaction to the highly unnerving few seconds that he had just passed through.

Much of Ole Devil's reaction was, he realized, stemming from a belated understanding of the possible effects of the risk he had taken. If he had been killed or injured, the very important mission upon which he was engaged would have ended in ignomonious failure.

And all because of a stupid act by a boy who might even be one of the party who were trying to prevent Old Devil from completing the assignment.

'Thanks, mister. You surely saved my life.'

The youngster's voice came to Ole Devil's ears as, starting to regain control of his churning emotions, he looked from the bear's body to where the linebacked dun had been brought to a halt by its trailing reins and was standing quietly. Something about the words, perhaps the fact that they sounded so damned effeminate, brought the young Texian's temper to boiling point.

'Why the hell did you have to pull such a god-damned stupid trick as that?' Ole Devil roared swinging around, fury making his features as Mephistophelian as 'Ole Nick' forking sinners into the fiery furnaces of Hades. 'Your folks shouldn't let you out alone if—'

The angry tirade died away at the sight which met the young Texian's gaze. And it wasn't the sight of the borrowed horse, carrying his sabre on its saddle, still galloping away that stopped him.

Having apparently contrived to wriggle onwards for several feet after falling down and losing his hat, the youngster had regained his feet. Returning the knife which he had been drawing to its fringed, Indian-made sheath, he was walking towards his rescuer. An expression of mingled relief and gratitude was on his tanned and freckled face as he held out his right hand.

The reason for the falsetto, effeminate tones which had been one cause of Ole Devil's annoyance was explained. Describing the youngster as 'he', or 'him' was most inaccurate. Despite the masculine clothing, the person he had rescued was a pretty and, although her garments did only a little to emphasize it, shapely girl in her late 'teens, with shortish, fiery red, curly hair. Her reaction to his hostile words and attitude suggested that the hair was matched by a hot and explosive temper.

Coming to a halt, her features lost their friendliness which was replaced by indignation. Like a flash, she whipped up her extended right hand in a slap that met Ole Devil's right cheek hard enough to snap his head around and caused him to jerk back a pace. Rocking to a stop and, in his surprise, dropping the

93

pistol he responded almost automatically to the blow. Before he could stop himself, he was launching a backhand swing in retaliation to the attack. Although he just managed to reduce the power behind it, as a realization of what he was doing belatedly came to him, his left knuckles came up against the side of her head in a cuff of some force.

The girl had been retreating. Her expressive features were registering a change to contrition, as if she was already regretting her hasty and uncalled for behaviour towards the man who had saved her life at some risk to his own. The blow connected, knocking her off balance. Staggering back a few paces, she flopped rump-foremost on the ground. A screech burst from her as she landed and her face turned red with fury.

Like the girl, Ole Devil started to regret what he had done. Meaning to apologize and help her to rise, he began to move forward. Before he could achieve either intention, she bounded to her feet. Ducking her head, she charged at him like a bighorn ram going at a rival in the mating season.

Growling an imprecation which he would not normally have used in the presence of a member of the opposite sex, the young Texian tried to fend off the girl. Although he caught her by the shoulders, the impetus of her charge drove him backwards. Unable to stop himself, or the girl, he retreated until his legs hit the now fortunately dead and motionless bear.

With the girl toppling after him, Ole Devil sat on the corpse. Pure chance rather than a deliberate intention caused him to guide the girl so that she landed face down across his lap. Studying the situation, he decided that the opportunity was too good to miss. Holding her in position by gripping the scruff of her neck with his left hand, he applied the flat palm of his right to the tightly stretched and well-filled seat of her buckskin trousers.

Ten times in rapid succession Ole Devil's hand came into sharp and, if the girl's yelps after each slap were anything to go on, painful contact with her rump. She struggled with considerable strength and violence, twisting her body and waving her legs, but to no avail. Suddenly, her captor once again realized what he was doing. He decided to bring the spanking, well-deserved as some might have said, to an end. Coming to his feet and releasing her neck, he precipitated her from his lap. She landing, rolling across the ground, and came to her knees.

Tears, caused by anger and indignation over the way she had been treated more than pain, trickled down the girl's reddened cheeks. She glared furiously at the young Texian as she sprang to her feet. Spitting out a string of curses which were the equal of any he had ever heard, she crouched as if meaning to throw herself at him for a second time. However, on this occasion, her right hand flew across to close around the hilt of the clip-pointed knife sheathed at the left side of her belt.

'I'm sorry that I spanked you,' Ole Devil said quietly. His soft spoken words were anything but gentle and, taken with the savage, almost demoniac aspect of his countenance, seemed to be charged with menace. 'But if you pull that damned knife on me, I'll take it from you and paddle your *bare* hide until you've learned better sense.

For a moment, watching the girl's every move and the play of emotions on her face, the young Texian thought that she intended to force him into a position where he would have to disarm her, even if he did not carry out the rest of his threat. She was quivering with temper over the humiliation she had suffered at his hands and made as if to continue drawing the weapon. Wanting to avoid such a confrontation, he stared straight into her eyes. Almost twenty seconds dragged by before she tore her gaze from his coldly threatening scrutiny.

'Just you wait until Grandpappy Ewart hears about this!' the girl warned, without looking at her assailant, spitting out the words as if they were burning her mouth. However, her fingers left the hilt of the knife.

'Who?' Ole Devil asked before he could stop himself, with a cold feeling hitting him in the pit of the stomach.

'Ewart Brindley, *fancy pants!*' the girl elaborated viciously, sensing her combined rescuer and assailant's perturbation and drawing the wrong conclusions regarding what had caused it. 'As soon as he hears what you've done to me, he'll skin you alive!'

'Diamond-Hitch Brindley!' Ole Devil thought bitterly, recollecting General Samuel Houston's comment on the advisability of keeping on the best of terms with the girl as that would be the most certain way of winning her irascible grandfather's support and assistance. 'I've sure picked a fine way of doing *that.*'

'Happen you know what's good for you,' the girl went on, although not quite so heatedly, when her warning failed to

95

evoke a verbal response or discernible change in the young Texian's attitude, 'you'll go catch my horse for me. Then get going to wherever you're headed and I'll forget what you did.'

Even as the wrathful words had been boiling from her lips, Charlotte Jane Martha Brindley was starting to regret that she was saying them. Always of a volatile and ebullient nature, she was quick to anger but just as ready to forgive; particularly when conscious that she herself was as much, perhaps even more, at fault than the other participant in the contretempts.

While Di had been very grateful for being saved from a very painful death, her rescuer's attitude and scathing words could not have come at a worse time. She had been churned up emotionally over her narrow escape and not a little annoyed by the realization that her perilous predicament had come about through her own reckless behaviour.

On finding the dead mule, which had strayed from the *remuda* the previous night, a girl with her experience ought to have shown greater caution. The *tobiano* gelding was not long broken to the saddle and she was riding it to further its training. So she should have known that it was not as steady as her regular horse and would be unreliable in an emergency. On top of that, when the bear had made its appearance, she had provoked a charge which could have been avoided by using her common-sense. In doing so, she had endangered her own and the stranger's lives. She could guess how he must have stopped the animal. Only a man of great courage, or a reckless fool would have attempted to do so in such a manner. Her instincts suggested that he came into the former category.

So Di's relief and gratitude had been entangled with guilt over her folly. Nor had her rescuer's behaviour on turning to face her done anything to lessen her emotional tensions. With her nerves stretched tight, his obvious anger had triggered off her unfortunate response.

Despite the way in which her rescuer had subsequently treated her, Di was sorry for the way in which she had acted. However, her pride would not permit an open apology and she hoped that he would do as she suggested.

For his part, Ole Devil could appreciate the girl's motives and, under different circumstances, he might have sympathized with her. Unfortunately, he too had been under a considerable strain and possessed a fair amount of pride. So her attitude was doing little to bring about a conciliatory situation. However, as he remembered what was at stake, he forced himself to consider how he might establish a more amicable relationship with her. He decided to explain what he was doing and hoped that she would have the good sense, sufficient gratitude for her rescue, and loyalty to Texas, to overlook the spanking.

Before Ole Devil could start putting his good intentions into practise, he saw four riders topping a ridge about half a mile away. One of them was pointing in his and the girl's direction, then they were urging their horses forward at a faster pace. He could tell that they were a Mexican and three buckskin-clad white men, two of whom were carrying rifles. While the distance was too great for him to make out further details, he was certain that they were the quartet he had been expecting to be in the vicinity. What was more, unless he was mistaken, the recognition had been mutual.

Ole Devil could have cursed the vagaries of fate. Having saved Di Brindley's life, which would have made him extremely popular with her grandfather, he had ruined the effect by giving her a not undeserved spanking. Now, before he could try to make amends, she was likely to find her life endangered because of him.

'Run and fetch my horse!' Old Devil ordered, striding forward. The urgency of the situation put an edge to his voice which, he realized too late, taken with his choice of words, would not enhance his popularity with the girl.

'Who the hell—!' Di began, once again taking umbrage at his tone.

The indignant tirade trailed off as Ole Devil hurried past the girl. Turning, she watched him picking up the pistol which he had dropped when she slapped his face. Then she noticed the approaching riders and stopped speaking.

Retrieving the weapon, Ole Devil examined it to make sure that its barrel had not become plugged up with soil when it landed. Satisfied, he replaced it in the belt loop and, after another glance at the four men, swung around. Much to his annoyance, he found that Di was still standing watching him.

'Get going!' Ole Devil commanded, bounding forward. 'Head for my horse!'

Realizing that the riders must be the cause of her rescuer's behaviour, Di did not waste time in asking questions or making protests. Turning, she started to run at his side. Any lingering doubts she might have been harbouring were wiped away when a bullet passed between them and ploughed into the ground a few feet away from the dun. She darted a glance at her rifle as she went by, but knew better than to stop and pick it up.

As Ole Devil was approaching the dun, he reached behind him with his left hand and raised the flap of the leather pouch that was attached to his belt. From it, he drew a rectangular metal bar with rounded ends. Having done so, he put on a spurt which carried him ahead of the girl. Arriving alongside his mount, he thrust his right hand towards the rifle in its saddle-boot.

'Mount up and get going!' the young Texian told the girl as he drew out the rifle and turned to face the direction from which they had come.

'Like hell I will!' Di answered, guessing what he had in mind. She pivoted to a stop by his side, reaching to haul the pistol from his belt's loop and, serious as she realized the situation must be, could not resist continuing, 'I hope whoever loaded this blasted thing for you knew what he was doing, fancy pants.'

'And I hope you know how to handle it and can shoot better than most women,' Ole Devil commented dryly, although he guessed that the girl would prove competent, accept that to try and enforce his demand for her to leave would be futile.

'I can shoot better than most *men*,' Di countered, speaking jerkily as she replenished her lungs with air. 'Don't worry, fancy pants, I'll protect you.'

While speaking, the girl was drawing back the hammer of the Manton pistol and gauging the strength of the trigger-pull that would be required from the amount of resistance she was meeting. It moved easily and the gentle clicking of the mechanism implied that the pull would be light, but not excessively so. Taken with the pistol's weight and balance, her deductions were comforting. She knew that she was holding a weapon of exceptional quality which, in capable hands, would prove extremely accurate.

Despite the danger which was threatening them, Ole Devil could not hold down an appreciative grin at Di's spirited response. A quick glance at her assured him that the breathless way she was speaking was caused by her exertions and not from fear or panic.

Having satisfied himself upon that not unimportant point,

the young Texian returned his attention to the four men. They had fanned out into a well-spaced line and were galloping closer. Although they still had at least a quarter of a mile to cover, the *vaquero* and the lanky man who had fled with him from the *cantina* were already holding pistols. Tucking his empty rifle between his left thigh and the saddle, the man who had fired the shot started to draw his handgun. However, the last of the quartet was still carrying a loaded rifle even though, as yet, he had not attempted to use it.

On meeting their companions, who had heard the shooting and were returning to the hamlet to investigate, Arnaldo Verde and Mucker had done almost exactly what Ole Devil had deduced they might.

Being aware that Al Soapy regarded every man of Mexican origin as a coward and knowing they had just as little regard for Mucker's courage, the *vaquero* had considered it advisable to stretch the truth when telling them what had happened at the *cantina*. So he, with Mucker's support, had deliberately overestimated the size of Ole Devil's escort. They had claimed that their quarry had been accompanied by at least half a dozen men and had appeared to have been expecting trouble, which had chilled any desire the other two might have felt towards avenging their dead companions.

There had been a difference of opinion between the quartet as to what their best line of action would be in view of the changed circumstances. Soapy had suggested that they should return to their hide-out and pick up reinforcements. Verde had pointed out that there had only been six men at it when they had left, and that their leader was intending to use them to gather together the rest of the gang ready to go and intercept the shipment. The *vaquero* had also pointed out that their task was to prevent Ole Devil Hardin from reaching Ewart Brindley and they would not have sufficient time to go to the hide-out before making another try at stopping him.

After Verde had established his points and gained his companions' grudging agreement, he had declared that they ought to continue with their assignment. As none of the others could come up with a better idea, they had let him make the arrangements. Without having realized it, the *vaquero* had duplicated Ole Devil's summation of the situation. Instead of trying to lay an ambush along the trail, or attempting to locate the young Texian as he made his way across country to Gonzales, they had headed directly to the town. Learning where the Brindleys' place was situated, they had taken up a position that offered them a good view of the terrain over which he was most likely to pass.

The discovery that Ole Devil was riding alone had been the cause of considerable recriminations, with Soapy demanding to be told what had happened to the escort. Although Verde had not cared for the other's attitude and implications, he had managed to control his temper. He had suggested that the men might have been accompanying the young Texian only as far as Guadalupe, or Gonzales. Or they might even have been a patrol which just happened to be using the trail and Ole Devil was riding with them for the company. Either explanation had left a number of questions unanswered, but the urgency of the situation had prevented them from being asked. As Mucker had said, no matter what had happened to the escort, its absence made their work that much easier and safer.

Accepting Mucker's statement, the quartet had set off to intercept the young Texian. Although while using Verde's telescope to watch for Ole Devil they had noticed Di Brindley, they had been in a hollow and missed seeing her meeting with him. On coming into view, having heard the shot, they had drawn at least one incorrect conclusion from the sight which had met their eyes. As they could not see the pistol which Ole Devil had discarded after firing, they assumed he was holding an empty weapon. So they had not been surprised when Ole Devil and the 'boy' – the quartet had fallen into the same error regarding Di's sex – turned and ran towards the line-backed dun. They had expected the fleeing pair to mount the horse and try to escape in that way.

Always boastful about his ability as a marksman, Soapy had tried to prevent the Texian and the 'boy' from escaping by shooting the dun. Not unexpectedly, as the range had been close to five hundred yards and he was sitting a fast-moving horse, he missed. So, having emptied his weapon to no purpose, he felt somewhat perturbed when Ole Devil and Di turned instead of mounting the waiting dun. If the way they were arming themselves meant anything, they were going to fight rather than try to escape with the animal carrying a double load.

Watching Ole Devil holding and doing something to the rifle which he could not make out, Verde did not share Soapy's misgivings. In fact he was not displeased by the way things were turning out. True the 'boy' had armed himself with the Texian's pistol, suggesting that it might have been reloaded, but even in skilled hands it would only be a short range weapon. The rifle which Ole Devil was raising to his shoulder would be a far greater danger.

'Keep moving at long range until he fires,' Verde called to his companions. 'Then rush him before he can reload.'

Although the *vaquero's* advice did not reach Di's ears, she was aware of such a danger. Having helped to fight off more than one Indian attack, she suspected that the four men might adopt similar tactics by hovering at a distance until fired on and then attacking before the empty weapons could be replenished. Noticing that her companion was taking aim, she decided to warn him against playing into the quartet's hands.

Before the girl could speak, the rifle cracked!

Almost as if wishing to oblige his attackers, Ole Devil sighted and touched off a shot. Soapy heard the bullet passing close to his head, but was not hit.

'Come on, *amigos*!' Verde yelled, watching the Texian lowering the rifle's butt so as to start reloading. 'We've got him now!'

CHAPTER TEN

KEEP GOING, IT'S EMPTY NOW!

EAGERLY urging their horses forward Arnaldo Verde and his three white companions began to close together as they bore down on their intended victims. Each of the quartet used his spurs as an encouragement to make his mount run faster, wanting to make sure that they arrived before the young Texian could reload his rifle.

Watching the men approaching, Diamond-Hitch Brindley was very worried and her earlier annoyance returned. She had been revising her opinion about the possible capabilities of her rescuer, deciding that he might be much less of the fancily-dressed dude she had first thought. After the way in which he had discharged his weapon's only bullet, she concluded that his method of dealing with the bear must have stemmed from ignorance and reckless folly and not out of a courageous calculation of the dangers it involved. There was, Di knew, no way that he could go through the time-consuming process of reloading any type of rifle with which she was acquainted before the quartet reached them.

That was where Di and the four men were making the same mistake. It was an error caused by ignorance, although pardonable under the circumstances.

At first sight, the weapon in Ole Devil Hardin's hands appeared to be a so-called 'Kentucky' rifle* of the kind which had long been popular in the more easterly of the United States; although it was being supplanted by the heavier calibred and shorter 'Mississippi' models west of that mighty river. However, a close examination would have revealed that it possessed several features which were not incorporated in the design of the standard 'Kentucky' flintlock, or the 'Mississippi' caplock. Most noticeable difference was the hammer being set underneath the rifle, just in front of the trigger-guard. There had

* The majority of 'Kentucky' rifles were made in Pennsylvania.

been a few 'under-hammer' pieces made, but they had never been common, or popular, due to the difficulty of retaining the priming powder in the frizzen pan. Neither had any of them carried a lever on the right side of the frame, nor had an aperture cut through it. An omission which might have aroused comment was a ramrod, for it was not supplied with the means to carry one beneath the barrel. The latter item was, in fact, not needed.

The action which Verde had noticed Ole Devil carrying out, but unfortunately for his party had failed to understand, was the remarkably easy process of loading a Browning Slide Repeating rifle. Once the original preparations had been made, it did not require a powder flask, patch, ball and ramrod.

The rectangular metal bar which Ole Devil had taken from the pouch on the rear of his belt was, in reality, the rifle's magazine. Five chambers had been drilled in the front of the bar, that having been the number Jonathan Browning had considered most suitable for convenient handling; although he produced models with a greater capacity if requested. Each chamber had a hole at the rear to take a percussion cap.

After firing a shot, a thrust with the right thumb on the lever caused the magazine to move through the aperture in the receiver so that the next chamber was in place. Not only did the mechanism lock the magazine into position, but thrust it forward until a gas-tight seal was formed against the bore of the barrel. As a further aid to ease of operation, the proximity of the hammer to the right forefinger allowed it to be cocked without the need to remove the butt from the shoulder.*

So Ole Devil did not have any need to reload in the normal fashion. Lowering the rifle as if he was compelled to had been done to make the quartet believe they had nothing to fear and to lure them closer.

When Verde and the three white men were about a hundred

* Despite the difficulty of transporting it with the magazine in position, Jonathan Browning had produced a comparatively simple repeating rifle that was capable of a continuous fire unequalled by contemporary weapons. For all its advantages, it never achieved the fame which it deserved. During the period when he was manufacturing it, between 1834 and '42, he lacked the facilities for large scale production. In later years he would have been able to do so, but the development of metallic cartridges and more compact, if less simple to construct, repeating arms had rendered it obsolete.

and fifty yards away, ignoring the muttering from the girl at his side – although he could hear that it consisted of profane comments about what she assumed to have been his stupidity in 'emptying' his weapon – the Texian returned the butt to his right shoulder. He had already pressed on the operating lever and watched the magazine creeping through the aperture. With all ready for aligning the sights, he manipulated the hammer with his right forefinger.

Sighting at Al along the forty and five-sixteenths of an inch octagonal barrel, Ole Devil selected him because his rifle was most probably unfired and, at that distance he would be the most dangerous of the four. Squeezing the trigger, the Texian felt the thrust of the recoil. Although smoke swirled briefly between them, his shooting instincts told him that he had held true.

Caught in the chest by a ·45 calibre bullet, Al was knocked backwards from his saddle and the rifle pirouetted out of his hand. The other three men were surprised that their intended victim had been able to fire as they had not seen him do anything which they could identify as recharging his weapon.

'What the hell—?' Soapy ejaculated, glaring from Verde to Mucker.

'It must have two barrels!' the *vaquero* answered, although he had a suspicion that was incorrect. 'Keep going, it's empty now!'

As double-barrelled rifles were not uncommon, Soapy and Mucker were inclined to accept Verde's solution. However, they were puzzled to see Ole Devil was still lining the rifle. So was the *vaquero*, but his thoughts on the matter ended in consternation as he realized that the strange weapon was being directed towards him. Before he could do anything to save himself, it spoke again. Shot in the head, he crumpled from his horse and was dead by the time his body struck the ground.

'What the hell kind of gun's that?' Mucker wailed, trying to slow down his racing horse.

'Come on!' Soapy ordered, being made of sterner stuff than his lanky companion. 'It must be empty now.'

Seeing that the last two men were not turning aside, as he had hoped they would, Ole Devil made ready to deal with them. He took no pleasure in what he was having to do, but knew he had no other choice. Not only were the approaching pair traitors to Texas, but neither of them would hesitate to kill him, or the girl, if they were given the chance. Should they capture the girl after disposing of him, her fate was likely to be worse than a quick death.

Operating the mechanism of the Browning, Ole Devil turned its barrel towards Soapy. While Mucker was doing as his companion had ordered, he showed less resolution and was allowing the other man to draw ahead.

Finding himself the object of their intended victim's attentions, Soapy thrust out and sighted his pistol as well as he could from the back of his galloping mount. He stood up on his stirrup irons, letting the empty rifle slip from under his leg, in an attempt to form a steadier base for his efforts. Fifty yards was a long range for a hand-gun, but he had seen sufficient of the Texian's marksmanship not to chance holding his fire until he was closer. The pistol bellowed and the sound coming so close to the horse's ear caused it to swerve.

Although the bullet threw up dirt between Old Devil's feet without harming him, the shot was not entirely wasted. Squeezing the rifle's trigger, he saw his target swing aside and, being too late to prevent the discharge, knew that he had missed.

Thrusting down on the lever with his right thumb, Ole Devil switched his aim to Mucker as the magazine crept onwards to position the final chamber in front of the barrel's bore. The lanky man might be allowing his companion to take the lead, but he still held a loaded weapon. Ignoring Soapy, the Texian turned loose his last available bullet. Attempting to steer his mount so as to put Soapy between them, Mucker caught the lead in his right shoulder. Screeching in agony, he lost his balance and toppled from the saddle.

That still left Soapy!

Seeing that he had missed with his pistol, he regained control of his horse and sent it tearing onwards. Hurling the empty weapon ahead of him, he saw Ole Devil fend it off with the barrel of the rifle. Reaching for one of the pistols which were hanging in their holsters from his saddlehorn, he knew that he would need time to open the flap and draw it. Guiding the horse straight at the Texian, so as to ride him down, Soapy hoped to gain it. Just a moment too late, he realized that the 'boy' was raising a pistol in both hands and lining it at him.

'Take him, Di!' Ole Devil yelled as he threw himself aside, hoping that the girl would at least be able to create a diversion.

Even as the Texian moved and shouted, he heard the deep-throated boom of a pistol. Looking up, he saw Soapy's head slam back and the hat flying from it. The speeding horse missed Ole Devil by inches as it passed between him and the girl. Its rider's lifeless body was already starting to slide from its back as it went by.

After glancing to where Mucker was sprawled face down and motionless, having been knocked unconscious when he landed from the fall, Ole Devil turned his gaze to Di. She was lowering the smoking Manton pistol and did not appear to be distressed, or even greatly concerned, by having had to kill a man.

However, as it had been because of him that her life had been endangered, the Texian doubted whether his standing with her grandfather would be improved.

CHAPTER ELEVEN

HE WANTS 'EM AND HE CAME FIRST

'GRANDPAPPY EWART, this here's Cap'n Hardin,' Diamond-Hitch Charlotte Jane Martha Brindley announced, leading the way into the sparsely furnished main room of her home. 'He's come over from San Antone with a message from General Sam—'

The introduction came to an end as the girl realized that her grandfather was not alone.

Without having waited to discuss what had happened, Di and Ole Devil Hardin had made sure that they had nothing further to fear from their attackers. Arnaldo Verde, Soapy and Al had all been dead. However, on examining Mucker, the girl had stated that, while he was still unconscious, his wound was not too serious and he would live. Then she had requested to be told why the quartet had attacked them, only now her opinion of Ole Devil was so improved that she spoke without making it a demand.

Noticing the change which had come over the girl, Ole Devil had given a full explanation. On learning that he believed the two attacks were attempts to prevent him from reaching her grandfather and being told the purpose of the visit, she had said they should question their captive on his recovery. Ole Devil had agreed that such would be their best line of action.

Looking a trifle sheepish, Di had thanked the Texian for saving her from the bear and he had returned the compliment with regard to Soapy. Neither of them had referred to the spanking which had been the unfortunate aftermath of her rescue. Instead, she had offered to have the men she would be sending from the ranch to collect the bear's carcass bring in the three bodies for burial at the same time.

Accepting the girl's offer, Ole Devil had agreed with her further suggestion that he went to see if he could catch some of the horses while she attended to Mucker's wound. On being asked if she would be safe, she had requested the means to reload the Manton pistol and, with it done, had declared that she could 'chill the ornery son-of-a-bitch's milk happen he woke up feeling feisty.' Confident that she could do so if it should become necessary, Ole Devil had mounted the dun and set off. Neither the horse he had been riding nor Di's *tobiano* gelding were in view, so he went after and succeeded in retrieving the mounts of the three white renegades. Verde's horse had been nowhere to be seen and he had not wasted time searching for it. On his return, he had found that Mucker was still unconscious but Di had done a very competent job of bandaging the wounded shoulder.

While they were waiting for Mucker to recover so that he could be questioned, Ole Devil had searched the bodies. He had found nothing, but put off an examination of their bed-rolls until he and the girl had arrived at her home. Di had gathered up the second Manton pistol and her rifle. On checking the latter to find out why it had failed her, she had concluded that the powder in the frizzen pan must have slipped away from the vent hole so that, when it was ignited, the flame had not reached the main charge in the barrel. After she had commented on the matter to Ole Devil, they had reached an amicable agreement about how they should address each other.

When Mucker had regained consciousness – he had been in a state of shock although neither of his captors had identified it by such a name – incoherent and unable to answer questions. Di had suggested that they took him back to the ranch and let him rest until the following morning. He had been barely able to sit his horse and had had to be tied on the saddle.

During the journey, Ole Devil had satisfied the girl's curiosity regarding the Browning rifle. They had also found his borrowed horse standing with its reins tangled in a bush. On arriving at the ranch, without having seen Di's *tobiano*, they discovered the corrals and barn to be deserted. Hearing a lot of noise from the cookshack, she had decided that the hired hands were having their suppers. Having no wish to disturb the men, she had suggested they should deliver Houston's message to her grandfather. Securing their prisoner had been no problem, even if his physical condition had been less enfeebled. The Brindleys' cook, an aged Tejas Indian called Waldo, occasionally went on a drinking bout. To prevent him from causing trouble – liquor had that effect on him – they had had a storeroom in the barn fitted with a sturdy door and strong iron bars at the window. Leaving the key in the lock – having placed Mucker on Waldo's bed – so that the cook could fetch him some coffee, Di had accompanied Ole Devil to the house.

Following the girl into the room, so that she could introduce him before going to make arrangements for feeding and guarding Mucker and having the bear and bodies collected, Ole Devil looked at the two men who were sitting on the only two remaining chairs at the table. He did not need to be told which of them was the girl's grandfather. Nor did he need to seek an explanation for the meagre nature of the furnishings. According to the girl, the majority of their portable property had already been sent to the east.

Ewart Brindley was not much taller than Di's five foot seven, but made up in breadth for what he lacked in height. Despite his age, he looked as hard and fit as a man much below his years. Almost bald, with his remaining hair a grizzled white, his leathery, sun-reddened face suggested not so much a bad temper but one which, like his granddaughter's, was quick and high. He was dressed in much the same way as the girl, with a bowie knife hanging from his belt. There was a spectacle case on the table in front of him.

Matching Ole Devil in height and build, the other occupant of the room would be in his mid-thirties, had dark brown hair and was suavely handsome. He was dressed in expensive, if travel-strained, riding clothes of the style much fancied by wealthy French Creoles in Louisiana. A shining black, silver-headed walking cane lay with his white 'planter's' hat on the table and he did not appear to be armed. He had stood up when Di entered, but had turned his gaze to Ole Devil when he had heard the name she mentioned.

'Howdy there,' Brindley greeted, his voice having a kind of high and harsh tone, also subjecting the young Texian to an interested scrutiny. 'What'd you say, Di – gal?'

'Cap'n Hardin's brought you a message from General Houston,' the girl answered, daring a curious and interrogatory glance at the handsome visitor. 'Set 'n' take the weight off your feet, mister—?'

'Now what'd General Sam be wanting from me, young feller?' Brindley inquired, ignoring what he had known to be his granddaughter's hint about the identity of the man at the table and the reason for his presence.

'It's a confidential matter, sir,' Ole Devil replied, flickering a look to where there other visitor was sitting.

'Happen you've come about using my mules,' Brindley drawled and jerked a thumb in the well-dressed visitor's direction. 'Mr. Galsworthy here, he wants 'em and he came first.'

Having delivered the information, the old man settled back on his chair and eyed the young Texian in a challenging fashion. Clearly he was waiting to discover how his news would be received.

Knowing that the correct response could be vital, Ole Devil thought fast. Possibly Brindley was anticipating a demand that the General's requirements should be given priority over private business. Or he might be expecting an appeal to his patriotism. Remembering Houston's comments regarding Brindley's contrary nature, Ole Devil felt certain that neither was the way to handle the situation.

'That's between you and Mr. Galsworthy, sir,' the Texian stated, meeting the old man's gaze without flinching and pleased with the opportunity to watch for evidence of how his words were being received. 'But I hope that you'll be willing to read the General's letter.'

'You couldn't ask for nothing fairer than that,' Brindley declared, although his face showed nothing of his feelings. He turned his eyes to the second visitor and went on, 'What do you reckon, Mr. Galsworthy?'

'Well, sir,' the handsome man replied and, despite his style of dress, he spoke with the accent of a well-educated citizen of Boston. There was a hint of icy arrogance in his voice, as if he was used to giving orders and having them carried out unhesitatingly. 'As I told you, my property is valuable and I'm willing to pay a high price to have it transported east. But, if General Houston needs your mules for some official purpose, I'm willing to withdraw any claim I might have on them. After all, the Republic of Texas must come first.'

'Be it official business they're wanted for, Cap'n Hardin?' Brindley asked.

'Yes, sir,' Ole Devil confirmed and gave his attention to Galsworthy, noticing that the other seemed to be avoiding looking him in the eyes. 'Thank you, sir. That's generous of you.'

'I'm merely doing my duty as I see it, captain,' Galsworthy answered and once again stood up. Taking his hat and cane from the table, he continued, 'As your business is confidential, I'll wait outside.'

'Ain't no call to sit out out on the porch, mister,' Brindley remarked. 'Hey, Di-gal, seeing's how Waldo's off feeding the boys, how's about taking this gent into the kitchen and giving him a cup of coffee while I find out what General Sam wants?'

'Sure thing,' the girl assented cheerfully. 'Come on, Mr. Galsworthy and I'll tend to it. You want I should fetch some in for you and Fancy Pants, Grandpappy Ewart?'

'How about it – cap'n?' Brindley asked, having turned a speculative gaze on the Texian when his granddaughter had used the sobriquet.

'I'd admire to take a cup, Miss Charlotte,' Ole Devil confirmed and watched the old man's head swivel rapidly between himself and Di in what would one day become known as a 'double take'. 'Black with sugar.'

'How many times do you want it stirred and shall I blow on it to cool it down?' the girl grinned. 'That's what you're used to, I'd reckon.'

'No, ma'am,' Ole Devil contradicted, watching Brindley's reaction to the by-play. 'My folks brought me up to be self-reliant and always made me blow on my own.'

'Allus did like a self-reliant feller,' Di drawled. 'Come on, Mr. Galsworthy.'

'Well I'll be hornswoggled!' Brindley ejaculated, after his granddaughter and Galsworthy had left the room closing the door behind them. 'She was like to bust the last feller's called her "Charlotte's" jaw-bone.'

'We came to an agreement soon after we met, sir,' Ole Devil explained cheerfully and truthfully, sensing that his host was impressed. 'Arranged that I wouldn't object to her calling me "Fancy Pants" once in a while and she'd let me use her given name in return.'

'Sit down, damn it, young feller,' Brindley requested and there was more than a hint of respect in his cracked old voice. 'Let's take a look at what Sam's got to be writing about.'

Reaching to the front of his shirt, as he took the seat which Galsworthy had vacated, Ole Devil produced a thin oilskin wallet from his inside pocket. Extracting the letter which Houston had given to him, he passed it to the old man. Brindley opened the flap of the envelope, took out the sheet of paper and spread it before him on the table. Then he removed the spectacles from the case and donned them. With his lips moving and silently mouthing the words, he started to read. On coming to the paragraph about Ole Devil, he lifted his eyes and looked at the object of the comments for a moment. Then he finished the letter.

'General Sam seems to set a whole lot of store on getting these rifles, young feller,' the old man commented as he removed his spectacles and leaned back.

'Yes, sir,' Ole Devil replied. 'Like he says, they could make a lot of difference when the time comes for us to take our stand against Santa Anna in open battle.'

'Likely,' Brindley grunted in a non-committal tone. 'How'd you aim to go about doing it?'

'Well, sir,' Ole Devil answered, sensing a challenge and selecting his words with care. 'Before I decide on that, I'd like to know whether you'd be willing to do as the General asks?'

'And just supposing I am?'

'Then the problem's at least partly solved, sir.'

'How do you mean, *partly* solved?' Brindley demanded. 'You reckon I can't handle it, or something?'

'No, sir,' Ole Devil assured his host, whose tone had been prickly with indignation. 'It's just that the situation has changed.'

'How?'

'The Mexicans know about the shipment.'

'The hell you say!' Brindley ejaculated. He glared at the letter, which had explained why it had not been felt necessary to send a military guard. 'How'd that happened?'

'I've no idea, sir,' Ole Devil confessed. 'The General and I were alone when we made the arrangements. We thought that as only he and I – or so we assumed – knew how I was hoping to make the collection, I wouldn't need a escort if you agreed to handle it. Then I was jumped by a bunch of renegades before I'd reached Guadalupe. We downed two, but the rest got away—'

'*We?*'

'I had a man with me, sir. But I sent him back to warn the General that there's a spy at his headquarters.'

'You did right there,' Brindley praised. 'It's something he should know. Are you sure that's why they jumped you?'

'Near enough, sir,' Ole Devil replied. While speaking, he had continued to watch his host's face. The examination was not particulary fruitful, for the leathery features were showing as little of Brindley's feelings as Houston's had during the earlier stages of the interview in his office. Which did nothing to make him more at ease as he realized that he was approaching the point where he would have to admit he had already placed the old timer's granddaughter in considerable danger. However, he also guessed that it would be advisable to let Brindley learn about the incident from him. 'The four who got away were waiting and jumped me just after I'd met Di.'

'They try *real* hard to do it?' the old man growled.

'Hard enough, sir,' Ole Devil confessed and, without elaborating upon the incident with the bear, described the fight that had followed the quartet's arrival. He finished by saying, 'I'm sorry it had to happen, sir, but Di had to kill the last of them—'

'You'd rather he'd've killed you, or her?'

'No, sir, but—'

'That fancy rifle of your'n was empty, way you told me, and she'd got your pistol?'

'Yes, sir.'

'Then somebody had to stop that jasper and she was the one best suited to do it, I'd reckon.'

'I'm not gainsaying that, sir,' Ole Devil replied. 'But Di's—'

'I've never figured she was a *man*, no matter how I've raised her,' Brindley interrupted and his harsh tones were strangely gentle. 'Boy, Di had to burn down a Comanche buck when she was fourteen. Eighteen months later, she blew half the head off a drunken *Chicano* 's'd got the notion of laying hands on her. 'Tween then 'n' now, she's been in three Injun attacks and done her share to finish 'em. Maybe that wouldn't be counted lady-like, nor even proper, back in the U.S. of A., but Texas's a long ways different. I've reared her to know how to defend herself. So I'm not holding it again' you 'cause she's had to do what I taught her.'

'Thank you, sir,' Ole Devil said sincerely.

'Do you reckon there's more of them varmints?' Brindley inquired, with the air of getting down to business.

'I'm not sure, sir,' Ole Devil answered. 'If there are, I'd have expected them all to be along after the first try had failed. The wounded man would know for sure, but he's in no condition to answer questions.'

8   113

'Maybe you didn't ask him the right way,' Brindley suggested.

'Maybe, sir,' Ole Devil conceded. 'But I think we'll get more out of him when he's rested, in his right mind, and has had time to think about his position.'

'Huh!' the old man grunted, but did not pursue the matter any further. 'Way I see it, we don't have too much time to get to Santa Cristobal Bay.'

'No, sir.'

'So how're *you* planning to handle the mule train?'

'I once tried to teach my grandmother how to suck eggs, sir,' Ole Devil drawled, having detected another challenge. 'She took a hickory-switch to my hide. One thing about me, I learn fast and easily – and it sticks once I've learned it.'

'What's that mean?' Brindley asked, although his attitude suggested he knew and approved.

'I'm just the General's messenger, sir,' Ole Devil replied. 'If he hadn't considered that you were competent to handle the collection, he'd never have suggested that I came.'

At that moment, the kitchen door was opened and Di entered. She was carrying a tray, with a sugar basin, milk jug and two steaming cups of coffee.

'Where's Mr. Galsworthy?' Brindley wanted to know when the man did not follow his granddaughter into the room.

'Just now gone,' the girl replied. 'Said to tell you "Good-bye and thanks for listening." Reckoned he'd head over to Gonzales and see if there was any other way he could get his gear shifted east. When do we pull out, Grandpappy Ewart?'

'How do you know we will be?' the old man demanded, accepting the cup which – having set the tray on the table – she was offering to him.

'Five hundred rifles, say ten pounds apiece; which I'd sooner go over than under,' Di remarked, half to herself and ignoring her grandfather's question as she passed the second cup to Ole Devil. Hooking her rump on the edge of the table, she screwed up her eyes and was clearly doing some mental calculations. 'Take 'em out of their boxes 'n' wrap 'em in rawhide, we could manage twenty-six to a mule. Be better at twenty-four though, which'll mean using twenty-one knobheads* for 'em. Another twenty to tote the ammunition. Fifty ought to be enough. Which's lucky, 'cause that's all we've got on hand.' Her gaze

* Knobhead: derogatory name for a mule.

flickered to the younger of her audience. 'What do you say?'

'You put the sugar in,' Ole Devil drawled. 'But you forgot to blow on it.'

'That mean you agree, or you don't?' Di challenged.

'I'd say that the agreeing to how it's to be done stands between yourself and your grandfather,' Ole Devil countered. 'What I could do, sir, is go to in to Gonzales and ask Colonel Gray if he can let us have enough men to act as escort to the Bay.'

'Why'd we need them?' Di asked, just a trifle indignantly.

'Those four renegades could have friends,' Ole Devil pointed out. 'And if they have, we'll most likely have them to content with.'

'I don't recollect's how Grandpappy Ewart 'n' me's ever needed to ask Lawyer Gray to do our fighting for us,' the girl protested. 'Nor anybody else, comes right down to it.'

'I'm not gainsaying *that*,' Ole Devil assured her. 'It's one of the reasons why I didn't bring men from San Antonio. But seeing how important our mission is and that we don't know for sure what we might run up against—'

'We've got a feller close by's could maybe help us on *that*,' Brindley pointed out, with the air of having solved their problem.

'Yes, sir,' Ole Devil agreed. 'If you want to go and question him—'

'Way he is, it wouldn't do a whole heap of good,' Di warned. 'I thought we'd decided to leave him until morning.'

'Sure we did,' Ole Devil conceded. 'But if you want us to—'

'I've not seen anything to make me think you pair don't know what you're doing,' answered Brindley, to whom the words had been directed. 'So I'll go along with it.'

'Anyways, sir,' Ole Devil drawled, not a little impressed by what he knew to be a compliment. 'I'll look in on him while I'm attending to my horses. Which I'd like to make a start at, if that's all right with you.'

'Go to it,' Brindley authorized.

'Can I take it that you'll collect the shipment for me, sir?' Ole Devil asked as he came to his feet.

'You can take it,' Brindley confirmed. 'We'll talk out the details over supper.'

Leaving the house, accompanied by Di, Ole Devil noticed

Galsworthy riding along the trail through the gathering darkness. Ignoring the departing man, they went to the barn. On unlocking and opening the storeroom, they found their prisoner was laying on the bed. Mucker was covered by a blanket and apparently sleeping.

'Shall I wake him?' Ole Devil inquired.

'I wouldn't, was I you,' the girl answered. 'Fellers I've seen took like he was when they'd been hurt got over it better if we let 'em sleep.'

'That's what I've found, too,' Ole Devil agreed and closed the door.

On their arrival to carry out the interrogation the following morning, Ole Devil and Di learned that they had been in a serious error regarding Mucker's condition. Going in to rouse him, they found that he had been stabbed through the heart with a thin-bladed weapon – and had been dead for several hours.

CHAPTER TWELVE

IT WAS MY FAULT, SIR

'SON-OF-A-BITCH!' Diamond-Hitch Brindley ejaculated, taking an involuntary step to the rear as she stared at the lifeless body on the bed. 'How the hell did this happen?'

'I'm more interested in who did it,' Ole Devil Hardin answered, studying the wound and taking note of the small amount of blood which had oozed from it. 'Because he sure as hell didn't do it himself.'

'None of *our* boys'd do it!' Di declared.

'I never thought they had,' Ole Devil assured her.

'Galsworthy!' the girl spat the name out.

'What about him?' Ole Devil inquired, although he had been considering the handsome man as a possible suspect.

'It must have been him!' Di stated.

'How did he know about this feller?' Ole Devil challenged.

'I – I told him!' Di admitted and, as the young Texian swung to face her, took on the attitude of defiance which he remembered from the previous afternoon. 'Hell, the walls of our place're so thin that he could hear what you and Grandpappy Ewart was saying. So I figured on stopping him listening and reckoned he'd be interested in hearing about them four fellers jumping us.'

'And as soon as you'd mentioned this feller, he said he'd be going,' Ole Devil guessed.

'Not *straight* after,' the girl contradicted. 'He finished his coffee, then asked if I reckoned Grandpappy'd do what the General wanted and I told him it was likely. So he said he'd head for Gonzales and see if he could make other arrangements.'

'You weren't to know what he was planning,' Ole Devil drawled. 'I'll say one thing, though. If it *was* him, he's a cool son-of-a-bitch. He must have come straight over here, let himself in, killed and covered this feller up and left, all within about five minutes.'

'We'd best go tell Grandpappy Ewart,' Di sighed.

'What've you got to tell me about?' Ewart Brindley's cracked tones inquired from outside the storeroom.

Turning, the girl and Ole Devil saw the old timer approaching across the barn. They stood aside and let him through. Then, after he had looked at the corpse, he turned his cold gaze upon them.

Although the young Texian met Brindley's scrutiny, he was far less at ease than showed on the surface. The previous night had done much to cement the amicable relationship that had been developing. Over supper, Di had told of how she had been saved from the bear. As he had been receiving the old man's gruff thanks, Ole Devil had sensed that the matter had cut deeper than heart-felt gratitude. Unless he was mistaken, Brindley had been impressed by the fact that he had not attempted to use the rescue as a means of attaining his ends. Nor had his prestige diminished when, after having eaten and made a fruitless search of the renegades' bed-rolls – which had been fetched from the barn by two of the hired hands who had said that the prisoner was still sleeping – he had spent an enjoyable evening in the company of his host and hostess. He had taken a lively and genuine interest in their arrangements for transporting the shipment, while also making it plain that he considered it was their concern and he would be merely an official passenger. In return, they had questioned him about the bid for independence and the state of affairs to the west. As they were supporters of Houston's policies, there had been no cause for controversy between them.

All in all, Ole Devil had gone to spread his bed-roll on the floor of the guestroom with a sense of achievement. His diplomatic handling of the Brindleys had, he felt sure, established the grounds for complete co-operation based on a mutual liking, trust and respect for each other's abilities.

Finding the man murdered, when they had hoped that he would supply them with vitally important information, might easily ruin all that had been achieved. However, Ole Devil knew what must be done.

'It was my fault, sir—' the young Texian began.

'No more'n mine!' Di interrupted and told Brindley what

had happened between herself and Galsworthy in the kitchen. 'Hell, I never thought—'

'Nope, and neither did either of us,' Brindley put in soothingly, glancing at Ole Devil as if in search of confirmation. After he had received a nod of agreement, he went on. 'I never took to that jasper, though. He never looked me straight in the eye when we was talking.'

'I noticed that, sir,' Ole Devil admitted. 'But I've known a few gambling men who wouldn't and that's what I took him to be.'

'And me,' Brindley declared. 'But it looks like he was tied in with them other four. Which fetches up another right puzzling point.'

'Why'd he come here?' Di concluded for her grandfather.

'That's the one, gal,' Brindley confirmed. 'Either of you smart young 'n's got the answer?'

'He was counting on them getting you, Devil,' Di suggested. 'So he came here to see if he could hire our mules and us to help him collect the shipment.'

'It's possible,' Ole Devil conceded. 'Did he tell you what he wanted moving, sir, or anything about himself?'

'Not a whole heap about either,' Brindley replied. 'He reckoned he'd come up from Victoria and had some supplies's he wanted to take east afore the Mexican army got there. Wasn't nothing about him to make me think otherwise. Anyways, you pair came in afore we could do much talking.'

'He must've been with those four yahoos when they first saw you, Devil,' Di guessed. 'Then headed here after he'd sent them to get you. I'd swear that he didn't know we'd fetched one of 'em in alive until I told him.'

'His hoss wasn't lathered when he got here,' Brindley comtented. 'Which it would've been had he come as fast's he'd of needed to if he had known. I reckon you could be right, Di-gal. Only, him saying he'd come from Victoria, it doesn't sound like he was after using the mules to collect the rifles.'

'He might have come to find out what he'd be up against if I should get by his men,' Ole Devil surmised. 'Or so that they could make you do what they wanted if I hadn't. You know, I couldn't help thinking yesterday that he didn't strike me as the kind of man who would give up as easily as he did when he found out that General Houston needed your mules.'

'He gave a good reason for doing it,' Brindley reminded his guest. 'A lot of folks, some's you wouldn't expect it from, are putting Texas afore themselves these days. Wasn't no reason why he shouldn't be.'

'God damn it to hell!' Di spat out furiously and indicated the body with an angry gesture. 'If we'd made him talk—'

'There was no way we could have, the state he was in,' Ole Devil pointed out.

'Even if it did come out wrong, you was both acting for the best by leaving him to sleep,' Brindley interposed. 'Anyways, there's not a whole heap of sense in crying over spilled milk. What we've got to do now is figure how we're going to play out the deal, way it's gone.'

'We could send Joe Galton and a couple of the boys after Galsworthy,' Di offered. 'A dude like him couldn't hide his sign so they can't find it.'

'He'll be long gone by now and might not be all that easy to find,' Ole Devil warned. 'Even if he is a dude, those four who were with him weren't and he could have more of them with range savvy. In fact, I'd bet on it. He must have been counting on us not finding out he'd killed the man until it was too dark for us to pick up his tracks. Which means he wasn't going to stay on the Gonzales trail. So he either knew he could find his way across country, or had somebody waiting who could.'

'I still say Joe and the boys could trail him,' Di insisted.

'Don't let me talk you out of the notion,' Ole Devil replied. 'It'll be a big help if we can find out just what we're up against.'

'I'll float my stick along of you on that, Devil,' Brindley drawled. 'Go and tell Joe, Di-gal.'

'Sure,' the girl answered, nodding to the corpse. 'I'll have him took out and buried while I'm at it.'

'Might's well,' Brindley agreed. 'It's got to be done.'

'You wouldn't change your mind about me going into Gonzales and asking Colonel Gray for an escort, would you sir?' Ole Devil inquired as he and the old man followed Di into the barn.

'That side of it's up to you, boy,' Brindley replied. 'But I'd sooner not. Like I said last night, all his men have families to move east. They'd not rest easy going off and leaving 'em to do it. Anyways, my boys've gone through Kiowa, Wichita and Comanche country 'n' come out of 'em all with their hair. So I reckon we could handle anything a bunch of white fellers try to pull on us.'

All of Ole Devil's last lingering anxieties left him as he listened to the first sentence of the answer. It implied that, despite the murder of their prisoner, the old man still respected Hardin's opinion and judgement.

'What I'll do,' Brindley continued, 'is have Tom Wolf and his boys ride with the train.'

'How about your place here, sir?' Ole Devil asked, being aware that his host had intended to leave half a dozen men as guards for the property.

'They couldn't have stopped the Mexicans burning it down, happen the army comes through this way,' Brindley answered. 'And there won't be all that damned much left for anybody to steal. So they'll be more use with us than sitting on their butts here.'

'We'll forget Colonel Gray then, sir,' Ole Devil stated, being satisfied that his host would not have reached such a decision if he had had doubts over their ability to manage without a military escort. 'From what I've seen of them, your men can take care of themselves.'

'You can count on it, boy,' Brindley grinned, pleased that his guest was showing such confidence in his men. 'They're not Mission Indians. Let's drift on out and see what's doing. I want to be moving out in an hour.'

Ole Devil's acceptance had not been made merely to please his host. All of the mule packers were Tejas Indians. However, he had noticed that they were lean, tough-looking men with an air of hardy self-reliance that made them very different from those members of their tribe who had fallen into the hands of the Spanish priests. That was one of the factors which was causing him to go along with Brindley's wishes. He also agreed with the old man that the escort soldiers from Colonel Gray would probably react unhappily at being taken away from their families at such a time.

Emerging from the barn, Ole Devil looked around. Not far away, Di was talking to Joe Galton. A tall, red-haired Texian of about twenty, dressed in buckskins, Galton was Brindley's adopted son and acted as *cargador** for the train. They had met the previous night, after Galton had returned from a successful hunt for camp meat. Ole Devil had found him quiet but

* Cargador: second-in-command and assistant pack-master.

friendly. Out of the *cargador's* hearing, Di had claimed he was not only good at his duties but was also an excellent farrier.

Turning as the girl walked away, Galton called two names and was joined by a pair of the Indians. They went to the corral, collected horses, and started to make ready for leaving. Going across to Galton, Ole Devil told him about Tommy Okasi and requested that if they met, the *cargador* would bring him to the pack train.

Having received Galton's promise on the matter, Ole Devil turned his attention to the preparations which were being made for the train's departure. While he had made use of a pack horse on more than one occasion, he had never before seen professional muleteers at work and found it interesting. There was a lot of apparently confused activity taking place, but it was all being carried out in a purposeful manner that told of long experience. Taking in all the sights, he realized that he was watching the cream of the mule-packing industry in action.

At General Houston's request, so as to prevent such fine animals from falling into the hands of the Mexican army, Brindley had sent the majority of his stock and hired hands to Washington-on-the-Brazos. It said much for the high esteem in which the normally fiercely independent old man held the General that he had retained the pick of his packers and mules in case they should be needed.

After a few minutes Old Devil became aware of Di's behaviour. Unlike her grandfather, who appeared to stay in the background and let the men carry on, she went from one group to another. Yet the Texian could see no reason for her doing it. The men were all obviously competent and did their work in a swift, capable manner. Suddenly she swung on her heel and came to stand at Ole Devil's side.

'Joe and the boys're on their way,' the girl remarked, nodding towards the corral. 'He says he'll catch up with us some time tomorrow, or later.'

'Huh huh!' Ole Devil replied, continuing to watch the work that was going on all around him. 'These men of yours are very good.'

'They should be,' Di answered, trying to sound off-handed but unable to conceal her pleasure at the compliment. 'Grandpappy Ewart trained each and every one of 'em. And don't you worry none, happen that Galsworthy *hombre* tries to jump us, you'll find they're just as good at fighting.'

'I've never doubted *that*,' Ole Devil assured her. 'Is there anything I can do to help?'

'Nope,' Di said and made as if to move away. Instead, she remained by him and went on, 'how much do you know about mule packing?'

'Not a whole heap,' Ole Devil confessed.

During the three-quarters of an hour that was needed to complete the preparations, Di told Ole Devil what was being done and why. In addition, she gave him much information about various aspects of handling a mule train when it was on the move. She talked all the time with a feverish zest, but not always in a smooth flow.

Before many minutes had passed, Ole Devil guessed what lay behind the girl's loquacity. Disturbed by the thought that she might never see her home again if the bid for independence failed or it should be destroyed by the Mexican army, she wanted something to take her mind off of leaving. So he listened and, when she showed signs of drying up, managed to find some fresh point upon which she could enlighten him.

At last everything was ready. Ole Devil noticed that Brindley's usually emotionless face showed that he too was feeling some strain over going away from his home. There was a catch in his voice as he gave the order to mount up and move out. Then, having swung astride his big *grulla** gelding, he gave his granddaughter a comforting smile. Having done so, he started the horse moving with the bell-mare stepping forward at its side. Hearing the tinkling of the bell, the mules surged into motion and the packers formed up about them.†

The day's journey was uneventful, except that Di rode ahead for a time. When Ole Devil caught up with her, there was evidence on her face that she had been crying. Neither of them ever referred to the fact that she had been in tears. However, the girl was anything but her usual cheery self as she continued to ride between Ole Devil and her grandfather.

The pack train was travelling with a scout ahead, one on each flank and two more bringing up the rear. At nightfall, Tom Wolf came in to say that he had seen nothing to suggest Galsworthy and his men were in the vicinity. Before going to sleep,

* Grulla: a bluish-grey horse much the same colour as a sandhill crane.

† The formation and organization of a mule train, including the function of the bell-mare is given in detail in: *Get Urrea*.

Ole Devil had the satisfaction of knowing that he was about twenty miles closer to his destination.

Moving on soon after dawn, the party progressed without incident until shortly after midday. While the animals were being rested, the Tejas packer who had been at the rear with Tom Wolf arrived with a warning that four riders were following them. Accompanied by Di, who was still disturbed and unhappy, Ole Devil returned with the man. They found there was no cause for alarm.

'It's Joe and the boys,' Di said, studying the four riders. 'Is that your man who's with them, Devil?'

'It is,' the Texian agreed, having identified the small figure who was leading a spare horse. 'That's Tommy Okasi. I wonder what he's got to tell us?'

CHAPTER THIRTEEN

I THINK SHE IS THEIR PRISONER

'TOMMY'S wig-wagging for us to catch up with him,' Diamond-Hitch Brindley remarked, pointing to where the little Oriental was sitting his bay gelding just below the top of a slope about a quarter of a mile ahead. 'Looks like there's something on the other side's he reckons we should see.'

'But we shouldn't let see us,' Ole Devil Hardin supplemented, taking notice of how Tonny Okasi was carefully avoiding showing himself to whatever – or whoever – was beyond the rim. Reaching down, he eased the Browning rifle from its saddleboot and, as he made ready to load it, nodded at the flintlock across the crook of the girl's left arm. 'Make sure that the powder hasn't shifted in the pan this time.'

'Yah!' Di scoffed, although she started to do as her companion suggested. 'At least I can carry mine ready to be used.'

Listening to the girl's response, Ole Devil was pleased to observe that she was more her usual cheerful self. She appeared to have thrown off the depression and gloom which had been caused by the thought of having left her home. It was clear that the decision to let her accompany Tommy and himself to Santa Cristobal Bay had been a wise one. It had come about because of the news which had been brought by Tommy and Joe Galton.

On learning that there must be a spy at his headquarters, General Houston had immediately started an investigation. However, the little Oriental had not waited to discover what had come of it.* Instead, armed with a written authority from the General, he had set out to rejoin Ole Devil. Riding relay

* The investigation was successful. On being told about the spy and asked if he had seen anything suspicious, First Sergeant Gladbeck remembered finding Juglares in the wine cellar and realized that it was directly beneath the General's office. Comparing the time at

and changing horses at Guadalupe and Gonzales, but keeping his bay with him, he had made very fast time. Meeting Galton and the Tejas, he had identified himself as the man Ole Devil was expecting and had accompanied them for the remainder of the journey.

While it had not been completely successful, Galton's mission had not proved a complete waste of time either. Without having produced definite confirmation, his findings implied that Galsworthy was not what he had pretended to be. What was more, despite his appearance, he had shown himself capable of covering his tracks along the route in which he was travelling. Even men as skilled as Galton and the two Tejas braves had had difficulty in following him. They had known that, as long as he kept moving, there was little chance of them catching up with him.

After having left the Gonzales trail about two miles from the Brindleys' ranch, Galsworthy had ridden west and met five companions at a small, deserted cabin. From there, the party had headed south. As they were swinging clear of the town, one of their number had left them to take a westerly direction. After covering about ten miles, Galton had stopped following them. They had shown no sign of altering their direction and he had considered that he would be more usefully occupied with the pack train.

Discussing Galton's information, Ole Devil and the Brindleys had decided that as long as Galsworthy had only four men with him he did not pose any direct threat to them. However, as he was travelling south, he might be making for a rendezvous with a force sent from the Mexican army. In which case, their position would be far more dangerous.

Taking into consideration the attempts upon his life and the fact that Galsworthy had sent a man to the west, Ole Devil had suggested that he might not have informed his employers about the shipment. If that should be so, he could be looking for assistance to deal with the situation. He was almost certain to

---

which Gladbeck had met the major domo with the information given in Ole Devil's report, Houston deduced that Juglares must be their man. So a trap had been laid. Calling Colonels Bowie and Travis in for a conference, Houston made sure that the major domo heard it would be one of considerable importance. He had been caught on top of the wine-rack and met the appropriate end for a spy.

be in possession of an identification document similar to the one which Ole Devil had taken from Halford's body. So he would have the means to enforce his request with any of Santa Anna's outfits that he came across. While it could prove serious, that possibility had not unduly alarmed Ole Devil and his companions. Unless Galsworthy or his men were fortunate enough to find the Mexicans in the next two days, he would reach Santa Cristobal Bay too late to prevent the shipment from being landed.

Having already explained the need to avoid the possibility of international repercussions, Ole Devil had warned his companions that the landing was the most critical period of the collection. Once the rifles were on shore and the ship had sailed, there was no way in which the Mexicans could prove that they had come from the United States. With that in mind, Ole Devil had proposed that he and Tommy should go ahead of the pack train at their best speed. When they reached Santa Cristobal Bay, they could make sure that there were neither Mexican troops nor Galsworthy and his renegades in the vicinity. If either should be around, they would find some way to alert the captain to the danger.

On her grandfather agreeing, Di had suggested that she should accompany Ole Devil and Tommy. Her argument had been that, if the ship arrived and there were no enemies present, she could help to prepare the rifles for being transported on the mules. They could, she had pointed out, remove the weapons from the crates and, using canvas and rope supplied by the captain of the ship, make them into bundles of a suitable size to be packed on the *aparejos.**

While conceding that the idea had merit, Brindley had suggested Galton or one of the men should go instead of his granddaughter. She had countered by reminding him that the *cargador's* secondary, but equally important, duties as farrier made him indispensable. If there should be fighting, any of the packers would be of more use than herself. Lastly, capable as he was in other directions, Ole Devil lacked the technical knowledge required to make up the bundles.

Intelligent and logical as the girl's reasoning had been, Ole Devil and her grandfather had realized that it had had a secondary motive. Ever since they had set off from the ranch, she

* Aparejo: type of pack saddle used for carrying heavy or awkwardly-shaped loads.

had been growing increasingly restless, moody and irritable. The cause of the change in her normally merry, happy-go-lucky disposition had not been difficult to surmise. While the train was travelling, due to the capability of the Tejas packers and the excellent training which the mules had received, there had been far too little requiring her attention and occupying her active mind. So she had had very little to divert her thoughts from the possible loss of the only home she had ever known. With that in mind, Brindley had acceded to her wishes.

Once again Ole Devil had considered that he was being given evidence of Brindley's faith in him. Having made the decision, apart from requesting that he took very good care of the girl, the old man had not shown the slightest apprehension or hesitation over letting her accompany him. Even though they would be travelling alone — apart from having his very loyal servant with them — for at least two and probably three days and nights, the latter being spent of necessity under the stars and far from other human beings, Brindley had obviously accepted that the young Texian would not attempt to take advantage of the situation.

Ole Devil had fully justified the old man's faith and trust. While possessing an eye for the ladies and being far from being a monk* (although he was not a promiscuous libertine) his sense of honour and duty had been effective barriers against him making advances to the girl. While aware of her physical charms, he had treated her as he would have a well-liked tomboy cousin.

Nor had Di given her companion cause to behave differently. Despite having grown up on the ranch, she was anything but innocent and naïve where sexual matters were concerned. Accompanying her grandfather on his packing trips had allowed her to travel extensively in and around Texas. Knowing the dangers, Brindley had considered it advisable to acquaint her with the facts of life. So, although she had been aware that Ole Devil was a virile, good looking young man, she had shown no indication of it. In fact, her behaviour towards him was almost identical to his own with regards to her.

Riding a two-horse relay required too much attention and effort for Di to be able to find time to brood about the possible fate of her home. She, Ole Devil and Tommy were covering

* The full story of why Ole Devil had to leave Louisiana may be told one day.

between thirty and thirty-five miles a day as opposed to the twenty-five maximum of the pack train. Although only the cook's and farrier's mules had been carrying a full load, Brindley had wanted to conserve the animals' strength for transporting the shipment. So he was maintaining an economical pace.

Apart from when answering the calls of nature, Di, Ole Devil and Tommy had made only one concession to her sex. On reaching the Navidad River about two miles south of the town of Edna, they had found the ford over which they had planned to make their crossing was far deeper than usual due to recent heavy rain. Wanting to save their clothing from being soaked, they had decided to go over wearing as little as possible. Without debating the matter, the girl had waited behind a clump of bushes while her companions undressed and made their way to the other side. Then, after they had gone out of sight, she had disrobed and followed them.

On making their plans for the journey, Ole Devil and the Brindleys had taken into consideration that Santa Anna had spies, or supporters, in most Texas communities. So they had decided to avoid such towns as lay between the ranch and their destination. As Di, Ole Devil and Tommy had by-passed Edna, so they swung around Matagorda. They were about five miles from Santa Cristobal Bay and had not seen any other human beings since leaving the pack train. Being so close to the rendezvous, Tommy had been ranging ahead as scout and now his actions suggested that there might be some kind of danger ahead.

Advancing cautiously, after having prepared their weapons, Di and Ole Devil joined Tommy who had withdrawn a little way below the top of the slope.

'Two Mexicans with a white woman, Devil-san,' the little Oriental reported. 'I think she is their prisoner.'

'Let's take a look,' Ole Devil suggested, slipping from his saddle and allowing the dun's reins to fall free.

Joining the young Texian on the ground, Di eased back the hammer of her flintlock and Tommy nocked an arrow to his bow's string. With the girl in the centre, they edged their way towards the rim. Crouching low, they peered over the top at the riders who had attracted Tommy's attention.

Even at a distance of something over a quarter of a mile, it seemed that the small Oriental's summation was correct. The woman, who was approaching from the direction of a large post oak grove, did not appear to be a free agent. Riding side-saddle on a good-looking black horse, she wore an expensive black riding habit that was somewhat dirty and dishevelled and a frilly bosomed white blouse. The brim of her head-dress – a masculine 'planter's' instead of the more usual top hat – prevented the watchers from making out the details of her face. However, they could see that her hands were either held or tied behind her back and that the horse was being led by a man at her right side. Well-mounted, clad in the fashion of working *vaqueros*, he and his companion were hard-looking Mexicans. In addition to a pistol and a knife on their belts, each of them had a rifle cradled across his knees.

Taking in the scene, Di let out an angry sniff. Always impulsive, she started to rise.

'Let's—!' she began.

'Keep down!' Ole Devil snapped, taking his left hand from the Browning rifle to catch her by the shoulder and enforce the command

'What the—' Di protested, but the very urgency of the Texian's behaviour caused her to obey.

'Old Nipponese saying, which I've just made up,' Tommy said quietly, bringing the girl's attention to him. 'Is foolish to try to rescue lady in distress if the way you do it gets her killed.'

'Hell, yes!' Di ejaculated and swung her gaze back to Ole Devil. 'I could have hit *my* man at that range, but you—'

'I don't think they saw you,' the Texian interrupted. 'So let's—'

Whatever Ole Devil intended to suggest would never be known. Even as he started speaking, they heard a feminine yell such as was used to encourage a horse to go faster. Next there came a shouted exclamation in Spanish, followed by the crack of a rifle shot.

Realizing that something must be happening to preclude the need for remaining concealed, Di and her companions rose. They found that, in some way, the woman had pulled the lead rope from the Mexican's hand and was galloping away from her captors. Smoke was drifting from the muzzle of the rifle in the hands of the man at the left. Clearly her actions had taken him by surprise. Despite being fired at what must have been very close range, the bullet had missed. At least, she was showing no sign of having been struck by it. She was not, however, out of danger. The other man was already raising his weapon.

Whipping the butt of the Browning to his shoulder, Ole Devil was conscious of the girl duplicating his actions. He sighted fast, knowing that he had a more distant mark at which to aim than the *vaquero*. Even as his finger tightened on the trigger, Di's flintlock roared. Ole Devil's shot sounded an instant after the girl's. One of them came very close to making a hit. The man's *sombrero* was torn from his head. Startled, he jerked the barrel of his rifle out of alignment and sent his bullet into the air.

Taking her right hand from the rifle and sending it flashing towards the powder horn and bullet pouch which were hanging at her left hip, Di allowed the butt to sink to the ground so as to reload. She saw that the Mexicans were staring in their direction and thought of the surprise that Ole Devil's repeating-fire weapon would hand them if they should attack or go after the woman. They did neither.

'*Vamos, amigo!*' yelled the man who had lost his hat, reining his horse around and putting his spurs to work, an example which his companion followed.

Watching the *vaqueros* racing off in the direction from which they had come, Ole Devil thumbed down the Browning's loading lever without requiring to think. He doubted whether there would be any need for the loaded cylinder which was moving into position. There was, however, something far more urgent requiring his attention.

Turning his gaze from the fleeting pair, Ole Devil looked at the woman. Her horse was galloping at an angle in front of his party's position. Riding side-saddle, with her hands tied behind her back, she had no way of controlling or halting the fast-moving animal.

'Here, Di, take mine!' Ole Devil ordered, thrusting the Browning rifle towards the girl. 'I'll go after her!'

Realizing what was expected of her, Di let go of the powder horn and her flintlock. Ignoring the empty weapon as it fell from her hand, she accepted the Browning. Ole Devil had taught her how to use it on the first night of their journey and she understood its mysteries. A glance assured her that he had made it ready to fire, the position of the magazine bar in the aperture supplying the information.

Confident that the girl could defend herself, or give him

131

covering fire if the *vaqueros* returned, Ole Devil turned and ran to the waiting horses. Catching hold of the dun's saddlehorn, he vaulted astride its back. He had gathered up the reins in passing and gave a jerk which liberated those of his reserve mount. Having done so, he sent the dun bounding forward.

'Go get her, Devil!' Di whooped as the Texian went by. 'I'll stop them from billing in.'

Urging his mount to go faster, Ole Devil heard the girl's encouraging words but did not attempt to acknowledge them. Instead, he concentrated his attention upon the woman and guided the dun at an angle which would bring them together.

'Look at that damned black go!' Di ejaculated. 'She's right lucky that she can ride so good the way it's running.'

Much the same thought was passing through Ole Devil's head as he was approaching the woman. Although the black was running at a gallop and, as he could see now, there was a rope knotted around her black gauntlet covered wrists, she was retaining her seat on the side-saddle with considerable skill. The jolting which she was receiving had caused the hat to slide from her brunette head and dangle by its *barbiquejo* on her shoulders. It allowed him his first unimpeded view of her face. Flushed by the pounding she was taking from the saddle, her features were beautiful. They topped what the riding habit could not conceal, a very shapely figure. She would, he guessed, be about Di's height and in her early thirties. However, there were other matters of even greater importance than her appearance to be considered.

With each successive sequence of the dun's galloping gait bearing him closer to the woman, Ole Devil started to think about how he might bring about the rescue. He discarded the idea of trying to come alongside and lift her from the saddle. Approaching as he was from her right, she had her legs hidden from his view. Having fastened her hands behind her back, the Mexicans might also have tied her feet to the stirrup as a means of securing her to the side-saddle. If so, he could throw the horses off balance and might even bring them down. Nor would there be time for him to go around and check whether she was tied on or not.

'Help!' the woman screeched, staring at the Texian. 'Stop the horse, *m'sieur!*'

Coming alongside the black, Ole Devil did not bother to reply to the woman's plea. Instead, he reached across towards the one-piece reins which were hanging over the horse's neck. Having obtained a hold on them, he cued the dun with knee-pressure so that it began to move off to the right. Feeling the pull on its bit, the black followed without making any fuss. Guiding the two animals around and gradually reducing their speed, he brought them to a halt in front of his companions.

'Nice going, Devil!' Di praised, having laid down the Browning after the Mexicans had disappeared into the grove of post oaks.

While speaking, the girl was advancing to hold the black's head. Dropping to the ground, Ole Devil went around the horses. He found that the woman's feet were not fastened to the stirrup iron. Holding out his hands, he helped her to slide down. She stumbled into his arms, causing them to tighten about her. Pressing – almost rubbing – her well-developed bosom against him, she began to babble incoherent thanks in a voice which had a marked French accent.

'You saved my life, m'sieur,' the woman stated, after recovering her composure and moving away from her rescuer. 'I don't know how to thank you.'

'Here,' Di said, stepping behind the woman. 'Let's get this rope off for you.'

On reaching for the rope, the girl noticed that it was tied around the stiff cuffs of the gauntlets. She gripped their fingers and pulled, liberating the woman's hands without the need to unfasten the knot.

Having been set free, the woman introduced herself as Madeline de Moreau. She explained how she had been the only passenger on a stagecoach heading for Texas City. It had been attacked by a gang of Mexican *bandidos*. The driver and the guard were both killed, but she had been saved from the same – or a worse – fate by being able to prove that her father was wealthy and would be willing to pay a high ransom for her safe return. The leader of the band had told the two men to escort her to their hideout while the rest went in search of fresh loot.

'A bunch of *bandidos*!' Di growled. 'That's all we need!'

'I don't think they will come looking for you,' Madeline replied. 'They were afraid of meeting soldiers and I'm sure that they believe there are more of you— There are more, aren't there?'

'Not too close,' Di warned. 'But they're coming.'

'Then you will be able to see me safely to Texas City, Captain Hardin,' the woman suggested, having learned her rescuers' names after introducing herself.

'I'll make arrangements to do it as soon as possible,' Ole Devil promised, but he could not shake off the feeling that something was wrong. 'But I'm on a mission of importance and great urgency and can't turn aside from it.'

'Very well,' Madeline said, accepting the situation without argument.

'If you feel up to riding, we'll move on,' the Texian requested, then his eyes went to the black. 'Hey! Where did they get the side-saddle?'

'It's mine,' Madeline answered. 'I had it with me on the coach and my horse was fastened to the boot, Would you help me up, please. I don't want to delay you.'

Complying with the woman's request, Ole Devil mounted the dun and retrieved his second horse. The party started moving and, as before, Tommy ranged ahead. In the late afternoon, as Ole Devil and the women were approaching a deserted building, they saw the little Oriental returning. They were about a mile from Santa Cristobal Bay, but could not see it as yet.

'There's a ship in the bay, Devil-san,' Tommy announced, bringing his horses to a stop.

'Is it the one we've come to meet?' Di inquired, although she sensed that the answer would be negative.

'No,' Tommy replied, confirming her suspicions. 'It's a small warship, flying the Mexican flag.'

CHAPTER FOURTEEN

YOU COULD BE TRYING TO TRICK ME

STANDING on the quarterdeck of the Mexican navy's ten-gun brig *Destructor*, having been called from his cabin by the master's mate who had the watch, Lieutenant Tomas Grivaljo directed his telescope at the cause of the summons. Three riders were coming down the slope towards the edge of Santa Cristobal Bay. They made no attempt to conceal their presence from the ship's working party who were refilling the water barrels at the stream which flowed into the sea at that point. The lack of concern was strange. The woman and the taller of the two men were *gringos* and their companion, who rode in a subordinate position behind them, appeared to be Chinese.

Puzzled by the trio's apparent lack of fear, Grivaljo studied the white man. Tall, young, unshaven, he had on a buckskin shirt and light-coloured trousers the legs of which hung outside his boots. There was a pistol and bowie knife balancing each other on his waist belt, but they were his only visible weapons.* A closer examination of the female suggested that 'girl' would be more appropriate than 'woman'. She was wearing a black hat like the man's, and a black riding habit but was sitting astride her horse. Neither she nor the small Oriental appeared to be armed.

Seeing that the working party were grabbing up weapons, the *gringo* raised his hands. He called something which Grivaljo, watching him, could not hear. Holding a pistol in one hand and cutlass in the other, the master's mate who was commanding the men on shore advanced warily. The trio brought their mounts to a halt. Still keeping his hands level with the sides of his head, the *gringo* swung his left leg up and over his dun's neck. Although he dropped to the ground, his companions remained in their saddles. Ignoring them, Grivaljo kept the

* As the use of a saddleboot as a means of carrying a rifle was not yet widely practiced, Grivaljo had not noticed the Browning.

gringo under observation as he strolled to meet the master's mate.

There was nothing in the *gringo*'s attitude to suggest that he had the slightest doubt about dismounting, thus leaving the means by which he might be able to make a rapid departure. Looking completely at ease, he walked a good thirty feet away from his horse and companions. Then, coming to a halt in front of the Mexican petty officer at a range where even a mediocre shot could be expected to make a hit with a pistol, he started to speak. Whatever the *gringo* was saying, he was apparently ready to back it up with some kind of document. Taking a sheet of paper from his pocket, he offered it to Master's Mate Gomez who opened it out and looked down at it. After reading whatever was on it, he pointed towards the ship. Then he handed back the document and he called to his men.

Turning to his companions, the *gringo* must have told them to dismount. Jumping from his horse, the small Oriental hurried to help the girl down. Then he held the animals reins while she joined the *gringo*. They spoke together and she seemed to be protesting. Instead of arguing, he pointed to one of the boats and she went towards it.

While the small Oriental led their horses towards the stream, the *gringo* helped the girl into the boat and then followed her in and sat by her side. Two of the sailors, looking disgruntled at having the task thrust upon them by Gomez, shoved the boat off, climbed aboard, and started to row towards *Destructor*.

Ever conscious of his dignity and having no desire to compromise it by showing his curiosity, Grivaljo lowered the telescope as the boat was approaching. Then he went to where he could watch without making his scrutiny too obvious.

On being brought alongside, the *gringo* showed that he had some knowledge of ships. Standing up, he took hold of the entering-ropes and hauled himself without any difficulty on to the deck. Several members of the crew were hovering around and, in fair Spanish, the *gringo* asked for help with the girl. There was a rush of volunteers such as Grivaljo had never seen on other occasions when the men were called upon to carry out some duty, but the bosun's bellow of displeasure drove them back. Having done so, the bosun and the *gringo* leaned over. The girl had risen nervously and, taking hold of her wrists, they heaved. With a startled yelp, she found herself being plucked from the boat. Her feet beat a tattoo against the side of the ship until she was set down on the deck.

Commanding the girl to come with him – and there was no other description for the way in which he addressed her – the *gringo* strolled nonchalantly to where Grivaljo was standing. As he approached, his eyes were darting around. Watching him, the lieutenant felt it was merely an interest in his surroundings that made him do so. There was nothing in his attitude to suggest he had any fear of coming to harm.

However, the girl did not appear to be quite so much at ease. That, Grivaljo told himself, could be caused because she was aboard a ship. Unless the lieutenant was mistaken, she was of a lower social standing than her escort. Her travel-stained riding habit was expensive, but it had been tailored to fit a woman with a somewhat more ample figure. What was more, if her tanned face and work-roughened hands were anything to go by, she had not always worn such expensive garments. Being a well-born Spanish-Creole, which accounted for his low rank and humble command, Grivaljo could guess at her relationship with the *gringo* and he dismissed her from his considerations.

Conscious of the lieutenant's scrutiny, Ole Devil Hardin forced himself to retain an outward calm and swaggering confidence. From the look of her when he told her to follow him, Diamond-Hitch Brindley was feeling the strain. Yet she had remembered to kick the sides of the ship while being lifted aboard, ensuring that if certain other sounds had been made, they would pass unnoticed. He felt sure that he could count on her to continue playing her part. If he had not been sure, he would never have allowed her to accompany him in the first place.

On hearing Tommy Okasi's news, Ole Devil had called a halt at the deserted cabin. Then he had discussed the matter with Di and the small Oriental. They had not attempted to exclude Madeline de Moreau from their council of war. While she had not been told the exact purpose of their assignment, she was aware that it was of considerable importance to the Republic of Texas. So she had taken a lively interest in what was being said.

While it had seemed likely that the brig was awaiting the arrival of the ship carrying the rifles, Ole Devil had pointed out that – as the crew were engaged in taking on water – it was possible the visit had only been made for such a purpose. One thing was obvious to them all. No matter what had brought the Mexican warship to Santa Cristobal Bay, its presence called for some kind of action on their part.

From all appearances, the owners of the cabin had left hurriedly. Certainly they had not waited to pack and carry off all of their property. Noticing one of the items that remained, Ole Devil had started to concoct an audacious scheme.

Telling Tommy to unpack his war bag, Old Devil had explained what he intended to do. Making use of the document which he had taken from Halford's body, he would visit the brig and try to find out why it was there. Should it be waiting in ambush, he would find some way of warning the arms ship of its presence. On the other hand, if the reason was merely to replenish the water supply, he had something else in mind. He would attempt to persuade the Mexican captain to sail south and, if successful, hoped to make sure that the brig would not be able to interfere with the landing of the arms.

On learning of how Ole Devil hoped to achieve his intention, Di had suggested that she should accompany him and Tommy. At first he had refused to consider the idea. However, as on the issue of riding with him to the Bay, she had had her way. Her argument had been that her presence might tend to lessen the Mexican's suspicions. Also, she had claimed, if Madeline would co-operate, she could carry the means to put Ole Devil's scheme into operation. Neither of the men would be able to do so, certainly not by concealing the object, and for it to be in plain sight was sure to arouse comments and questions.

On Ole Devil yielding to Di's demands, Madeline had suggested that she too should accompany the party. The girl had replied that she did not think it would be a good idea, as there would be considerable danger involved and the need for fighting or fast movement. Di had not considered the woman capable of either, but thought she could help in another way. Madeline had accepted the girl's decision with apparent good grace. At any rate she had not hesitated to agree when the girl asked to change clothes with her. Nor had the woman shown any alarm over being left alone at the cabin. She had stated that she was a pretty good shot and would have a selection of firearms at her disposal should the need to prove it arise.

With the various points settled, the party had made their preparations. In addition to having changed his riding breeches for less military-looking trousers from his war bag, Ole Devil had left his second pistol and sabre – which had his name inscribed on the blade – at the cabin.

For the part which she would be playing, Di could not carry her rifle. Taking advantage of the riding habit's slightly loose fit, she had buckled her belt around her underwear and had concealed the secret object beneath the outer garment. She had, however, insisted upon riding astride as she had never used a side-saddle.

Wanting to appear innocuous and to be more convincing in his pose of a harmless 'Chinese' servant, Tommy had left his bow, arrows and swords behind, as well as changing his boots for a pair of sandals. He had, however, retained one weapon; but few people outside his native land would have identified it as such. Certainly Madeline, who had seen him replacing it in his trousers' pocket after having shown it to a clearly puzzled Di, had not. Nor had she heard the explanation of its purpose as that had been made while the trio were riding towards the rendezvous.

Before allowing themselves to be seen, Di, Ole Devil and Tommy had studied the brig as it lay at anchor. It was, the Texian had told the girl, well-situated for ambushing any vessel that entered. Due to the way in which the land rose on three sides, it could only be seen from the sea when the mouth of the bay was being approached. At night, provided that the brig was properly darkened, it would be practically invisible against such a background. However, the precautions which Hardin expected had not been taken. There was no lookout on either of the mastheads. The breechings and side-tackles had not been cast off, nor the guns run out. Neither was there a spring attached to the anchor's cable to facilitate turning the brig and bringing one of its broadsides to bear.

Ole Devil had regarded the lack of preparations as a good sign. Unless he was mistaken, the omissions were not the result of incompetence. To his eyes, the brig showed no signs of being poorly commanded. In fact he had concluded it was just the opposite. Although the party on shore had been working in a somewhat dilatory fashion, he believed that could be the fault of the master's mate who was in charge rather than the captain.

The lieutenant, whom Ole Devil was approaching, seemed old for such a low rank, particularly as he had the appearance of being a capable seaman. There was a bitter expression on his lean, aquiline face that the Texian recognized as common to officers in other navies who had, for some reason, been passed over for promotion.

'*Saludos, senor*,' Ole Devil greeted, taking out the 'proof' of his identity. His bearing suggested that he was merely going through an unnecessary formality. 'This will tell you who I am.'

'Well, *Senor* Halford,' Grivaljo said, after reading the document and introducing himself. 'What brings you to my ship?'

The voice suggested to Ole Devil why Grivaljo was still only a lieutenant. Some of the Spanish warships and their crews had gone over to the Mexicans during the struggle for independence, as had military units. According to rumours, officers of Spanish-Creole birth were discriminated against by their Mexican superiors. If that was so in Grivaljo's case, dealing with him could be easier.

'Information, lieutenant,' Ole Devil replied, accepting and refolding the document. 'Something you'll be pleased to hear about.'

'Will I?' Grivaljo asked.

'If you've a mind to make some prize money, you will,' Ole Devil answered in a louder voice than was necessary.

'Prize money?' Grivaljo repeated. Then, hearing his words echoed in a number of voices, he realized that the conversation was being listened to by almost every man on deck. Angrily, he raised his voice in a bellow. 'Bosun! Put the hands to work, damn you!'

'Like I said, if you've a mind for prize money, you'll be pleased to hear what we've found out,' Ole Devil stated, as the cursing bosun chased the sailors away.

'*We, senor?*' Grivaljo said quietly, keeping his eyes on the Texian's face. 'And who might "*we*" be?'

'The people I work with.'

'Who are they?'

'Friends of Mexico,' Ole Devil countered. 'I don't give names. Right now, I'm taking a pretty important message to General Rovira. But my boss told me to keep close to the coast and get word to any Mexican warship I saw going by that there's a ship expected during the next three days at Port Lavaca.' He paused dramatically, then continued, 'It's carrying supplies for Houston – including ten thousand Yankee dollars.'

'How do you know of this?' Grivaljo demanded, trying, and not entirely succeeding, to sound disinterested.

'Come on now! A man of your intelligence doesn't really expect me to give the answer to *that*,' Ole Devil scoffed, with the air of one who had done his duty. 'Well, I've told you. The news I've got for General Rovira's important, so I'll be on my way and let him have it.'

'Just a moment, *senor*!' Grivaljo barked as his visitor went to turn away. 'It's not as easy as all that. You could be trying to trick me.'

'Even if *I'd* come out here instead of just sending a message with one of your men,' Ole Devil countered calmly. 'Would I have brought my girl along if that's what I had in mind?'

'Perhaps not,' Grivaljo answered, although a similar thought had occurred to him. 'But—'

'There are no "buts" about it where I'm concerned!' Ole Devil interrupted, bristling with well-simulated indignation. 'Damn it all, I've told you something that any naval officer ought to be pleased to know. If you don't want to believe me and act on it, that's up to you. I'll be going—'

'Not so fast!' Grivaljo snapped. Although he was not armed, he felt sure that the *gringo* would have more sense than to attempt resistance. 'Being, as you said, a man of intelligence, I think it would be better if you stayed on board until after I've seen this ship which you *say* is bound for Port Lavaca.'

'As I'm here, and seeing that the boat which brought me's gone back, I'd be a fool to try and stop you,' Ole Devil declared, giving a resigned shrug. He showed nothing of the elation that he was feeling. From the way he had spoken, the lieutenant was contemplating acting upon Hardin's information, which suggested that he was not awaiting the arrival of the consignment of rifles. Looking Grivaljo straight in the eye, he went on, 'But I want what you're doing put in writing, so that I can show General Rovira what's made me late getting to him.'

'What do you mean?' the lieutenant asked uneasily, showing that he had a pretty fair idea of the answer.

'Like I told you,' Ole Devil drawled. 'I've some *very* important news for the General. Getting it to him, even with her—' He indicated the girl with a disparaging jerk of his left thumb, 'and my "Chink" servant along to make folks less suspicious – don't worry, she's so stupid she barely speaks English

141

and doesn't know a word of Spanish – it's going to be dangerous to deliver. So, if I'm going to be delayed maybe two or three days – there's no way of knowing just when that ship will arrive – I want to be able to prove *I* wasn't responsible.'

Listening to the conversation, Di – who spoke sufficient Spanish to follow it – silently swore that she would raise lumps on a certain Texian's head for his comment about her. However, impressed as she was by the way Ole Devil was manipulating the officer, she did not forget her part. Standing with a partially open mouth and an expression that suggested a complete lack of comprehension, she showed none of her admiration for Ole Devil's acting. Everything about him implied that he was completely content to be delayed – as long as he could lay the blame on somebody else.

Watching Grivaljo's reactions, Ole Devil could guess at the cause of his perturbation. While one part of the lieutentnat advised taking the precaution of keeping Hardin on board, another was warning him of the consequences if he should do so and be proven wrong. General Rovira was one of the new breed of Mexican – as opposed to Spanish-*Creole* – officers. The kind of man, in fact, who had probably blocked Grivaljo's promotion because of his birth and upbringing. If Rovira learned that vital information had been prevented from reaching him as quickly as possible, he would have no mercy on the man – especially upon a *Creole* – who had caused the delay.

'Don't get any ideas about holding me until you're sure, then having me disappear and saying you've never seen me,' Ole Devil warned, seeing from Grivaljo's expression that such an idea was at that moment being contemplated. 'For one thing, some of the crew would talk. And even if they didn't, unless that "Chink" of mine gets a signal from me that all's well in about a minute, he'll be on his horse and heading back to tell my boss where I am. Maybe he's only a heathen Chinese, but he could do it.'

An angry scowl creased the lieutenant's face and his fingers drummed against his thighs. He had already considered the first objection – that of an indiscreet crew suggested by the *gringo*. While he did not believe it to be insurmountable, the second point put his plan beyond any hope of accomplishment. Even if he clapped his visitors below hatches immediately and sent a flag signal to the shore party, the 'Chinaman' would almost certainly take fright and flee. He was far enough away from the sailors to mount and be reasonably safe from their pistols. For the *gringo* to have adopted such a high-handed attitude implied that he had very influential superiors. In all probablity, they would be men who could cause a great deal of trouble over his disappearance. It would go badly for any officer who was suspected of being involved, particularly if he was a Spanish-*Creole.*

Unpalatable as the thought might be, Grivaljo had to accept that he could not impose his will upon the sardonic-looking young white man.

'Very well, signal your man that all is well,' the lieutenant requested, almost spitting each word out in the bitterness of defeat. 'I'll have you put ashore as soon as the boats come back.'

'*Gracias,*' Ole Devil replied, although the latter part of the officer's speech did not fit into his plans. 'And you'll go after that ship?'

'I'll sail with the morning tide,' Grivaljo promised and could not stop himself from adding, 'For a "friend of Mexico", you don't have much faith in your friends.'

'I was born careful,' Ole Devil answered. 'Which is why I like to choose the winning side. Especially when it's the side who can pay best.'

'How do you mean?' the lieutenant wanted to know.

'I'm not so *loco* that I believe *el Presidente* will let any *gringo*, even those who have stood by him, stay on in Texas,' Ole Devil explained. 'So I'm making sure I don't leave with empty pockets.'

'Hey, honey,' Di put in, speaking English with a whining tone. 'How much longer you going to stand a-jawing? I'm hungry 'n' tired, although I'm damned if I know what we'll eat tonight. You ain't shot noth—'

'Shut your mouth, damn you!' Ole Devil snarled in the same tongue, swinging around to face the girl, and she backed off a couple of steps registering right in a convincing manner. He turned back to the officer and, although he sensed that the other understood sufficient of the language to have followed the brief conversation, he reverted to Spanish. 'She's right, though. We've been travelling so hard I haven't had time to shoot anything. How about trading a meal for the news I've brought?'

'Very well,' Grivaljo answered, after a pause during which

he revised his original inclination to refuse. It might, he realized, be impolitic to antagonize a man with possible influential connections, one who could maybe supply information in the future. 'I was just going to ask you to be my guest.'

'That's good of you,' Ole Devil declared, adopting a more friendly tone and feeling delighted at the way the officer had played into his hands. There was one more thing which had to be arranged. 'Can I have my "Chink" come out and eat?'

'Of course. I'll pass the word for the shore party to bring him,' Grivaljo assented and nodded up at the rapidly darkening sky. 'It looks like rain. Perhaps you and your – wife – would like to spend the night on board and shelter from it?'

'We'd be pleased to,' Ole Devil replied, showing nothing of his delight at the suggestion – upon which the success of his plan depended – having come from the other man. 'Just so long as we can get off again *before* you sail.'

'I'll have you put ashore at first light,' Grivaljo promised. 'You have my word of honour as an officer and gentleman.'

The acceptance was made with almost good grace. As far as the lieutenant could tell, he had nothing to lose by being amiable to his *gringo* visitors.

In that, Grivaljo was making a very serious mistake!

It was one which was to have a severe effect on his career!

CHAPTER FIFTEEN

IF YOU DON'T WANT TO GET HER KILLED

'WHEN do you reckon it'll happen, Devil?' Diamond-Hitch Brindley inquired as she sat her horse between her companions and watched the *Destructor* brig sailing out of Santa Cristobal Bay shortly after dawn on a cold, miserable and – although the rain had stopped – damp morning.

'Not until they set all sail and hit the rough water,' Ole Devil Hardin replied. 'Unless they find out what's happened before then.'

'If they do,' Di said, turning a sympathetic eye on the other member of their party. 'You'll have had a wet night for nothing.'

Even though the girl spoke lightly she knew that the failure of their plan might have more serious repercussions than the waste of Tommy's night in considerable discomfort and not a little danger.

On receiving Ole Devil's message, which Lieutenant Grivaljo had sent ashore, Tommy had off-saddled and hobbled the horses. When he had reached the brig, he was given a meal. As the vessel was already crowded, he had been told to make himself a shelter between two of the starboard side's twenty-four pounder carronades.* That had been ideal for his purpose, having given him a legitimate reason for staying on deck. He could keep watch in case the ship carrying the rifles should arrive and, if it had, contrive to give a warning of the danger. More important, it had allowed him to carry out another task.

Despite the discomfort it had caused, the rain which had fallen steadily for most of the night had been of great help to Tommy. On the pretense of collecting something from her saddlebags, their property having been brought on board by the

* Carronade: a short-barrelled, large calibre, compact cannon with a limited range used as a broadside weapon on some classes of warship.

brig's shore party, Di had given him the saw which they had found at the cabin. She had been carrying it suspended from her belt and under the borrowed riding habit.

Once satisfied that Grivaljo had turned in, the master's mate who had the watch did not remain on deck. He went below to shelter from the rain. So, once he had left, so had the other members of the watch. In their absence, working with more freedom than would have been possible if they had attended to their duties Tommy had started to work. Using the saw, which was practically new, he had cut into the breeching, side-tackles and the lashing which held the muzzle of each carronade against the top of its gun-port.

The departure of the sailors had allowed Tommy to work with less immediate danger of being caught. Taking his time, he had worked on the inner sides of the various ropes so as to lessen the chances of his tampering being discovered prematurely. He had not, of course, sawn all the way through. To have done so would have made the damage so obvious that it could not be missed. Instead, he had weakened the ropes. He had sought for the happy medium of cutting just deep enough to ensure that they would not start breaking until the brig was well clear of the bay. So well had he done the preliminary work that he and his company had been put ashore and the brig had set sail without it having been noticed.

Although just as interested as the girl, Ole Devil and Tommy hid their feelings better. She was wriggling impatiently in her saddle and staring at the brig with grim concentration. While she had little knowledge of ships, when she saw the additional sails being unfurled as it passed beyond the mouth of the bay, she turned her head and grinned expectantly at her companions before resuming her scrutiny.

Nothing untoward happened.

Carried onwards by the shore-breeze, *Destructor* heeled over and turned to the south. Despite being rolled by the waves, it kept going without showing any evidence of distress.

'Damn it!' Di ejaculated after about five restless minutes had dragged by, 'They must have found out!'

'I don't think so,' Ole Devil contradicted, trying to conceal his disappointment. 'They'd be reducing sail if they had, or turning back so that they could make repairs in the bay.'

'Those ropes must have been of better quality than I

146

thought,' Tommy commented in tones of contrition. 'Or I didn't saw into them as deeply as I thought I was doing.'

Whatever the reason, the brig was still under all sail and clearly not in any difficulties when it disappeared beyond the horizon. The only slight satisfaction Ole Devil could find was that it had not shown any signs of returning.

Di could not hide her disappointment as she turned her horses. However, being a good natured girl, she felt that she should prove to Tommy that she did not hold the failure against him.

'You wouldn't be able to see in the dark and sure as hell couldn't't've started lighting matches even if it hadn't been raining,' Di stated as they rode away from the rim overlooking the bay. 'Anyways, we got the damned thing headed south and that's almost worth having to wear this son-of-a-bitching riding habit for. What do you reckon Grivaljo'll do when he finds out, Devil?'

'That depends,' the Texian answered, having given the matter some consideration. 'He may think we went aboard just to do the damage and put the brig out of action, But, if he decides that we'd need a better inducement than *that* before taking such a risk, he could guess we wanted him gone because we're expecting a ship to arrive.'

'And if he does,' Di said bitterly, 'he'll be headed right back.' Then her face showed relief and she went on, 'Hey though. He can't. The wind's blowing him south.'

'That won't stop him,' Ole Devil warned, but he did not attempt to explain how a sailing ship could beat back against the wind. Instead, he gave a shrug. 'Well, there's nothing we can do about it right now. So we might as well go back and let you get into your own clothes.'

'I sure as hell won't be sorry about *that*!' Di spat out, trying to pass off her unrealized hopes and present anxieties as lightly as possible

All in all, it was a dejected trio who rode towards the cabin. Yet, although they did not learn of it for many weeks, their plan met with complete – if belated – success.*

In spite of their gloomy forebodings, Di, Ole Devil and Tommy did not forget to be cautious. However, they saw nothing to disturb or perturb them as they approached the

* Details of how this came about are given at the end of this chapter.

building. It had been erected in the centre of a fair-sized hollow, with plenty of open ground on every side to counteract the clumps of trees and bushes which grew thickly in a number of places. There was no sign of life, but that was neither surprising nor alarming. To prevent drawing attention to the fact that the cabin was occupied, they had taken Madeline de Moreau's black gelding with them. Ole Devil had also asked the woman to stay indoors as much as possible.

Taking the horses to the small corral, the trio dismounted. They were about to start attending to the animals' welfare when the side door of the cabin was opened. Expecting no more than Madeline coming out to greet them, Ole Devil glanced over his shoulder. He stiffened and his right hand went towards the butt of the Manton pistol. Hearing Di's low and startled exclamation, he knew without turning his head that she was also looking. There was a very good reason for their reactions.

Although Madeline was emerging, clad in Di's shirt and trousers – which were tight enough to show off her full figure to its best advantage – she was not alone. Walking close behind her, with the muzzle of a pistol held against the side of her head, was the man who had called himself 'Galsworthy' when he had visited the Brindleys' ranch. His other hand, holding the walking-cane which Ole Devil had already suspected was concealing the blade of the sword that had murdered the wounded prisoner, was resting on her shoulder and urging her onwards.

'Come away from those horses!' Galsworthy barked, pushing Madeline forward.

'D – Do it, please!' Madeline gasped in a frightened voice.

'You'd better, if you don't want to get her killed,' Galsworthy supplemented. 'And don't think I – wouldn't shoot a woman.'

'Do as he says!' Ole Devil ordered, having no doubt that the man was not making an idle threat.

Even as he spoke, the young Texian was trying to locate Galsworthy's companions. It was unlikely that he had left the other men with their horses. The nearest point at which they and the animals could be concealed was almost two hundred yards away, too far for them to be of use in an emergency. So, in all probability, they would be in the cabin. They were either positioned so as to be able to cover their leader, or were waiting to follow him out.

'Stop there!' Galsworthy commanded when the trio had moved far enough for them to be unable to use the horses as a shield. They did as they were told and he went on, 'Now throw down your weapons. Do it carefully and no tricks, or she's dead.'

Knowing that he had no other choice without costing Madeline her life, Ole Devil extracted the pistol from his belt loop. He tossed it in front of him so that it landed on its left side with the hammer uppermost. Having done so, he slid the bowie knife from its sheath and flipped it point first into the ground alongside the other weapon.

'How about you and the "Chink"?' Galsworthy asked, looking at Di.

'Neither of them are armed, Randy,' Madeline said, before the girl could reply. Then she stepped away from the man.

'What the—?' Di spluttered, then realization struck and her voice rose like the squall of an angry bobcat. 'Why you—!'

'Easy!' Ole Devil snapped, catching the furious girl by the arm as she was about to spring forward. 'That won't do any good!'

Much to Ole Devil's relief, Di restrained her impulse. She might be hot-tempered, but she had enough sense to recognize sound advice when she heard it. Now she realized that the way in which Madeline's clenched fists had been raised was not that of a frightened woman, and she also saw the two men who were coming out of the cabin. Although she had not had a close acquaintance with them, she identified them as the Mexicans who had been Madeline's 'captors'. Grinning at each other, they went to flank Galsworthy and the woman. Clearly the pair were satisfied that the situation was under control. While each was holding a pistol, the muzzles were dangling towards the ground.

'It's lucky for you that you stopped,' Galsworthy told the girl with a grin. Then he swung his pistol, which had been pointing towards Ole Devil, in Tommy's direction and snarled, 'Bring it out empty, damn you!'

'Very sorry, sir!' the little Oriental yelped, snatching his right hand from his trousers' pocket into which he had slipped it. However, his hand did not emerge quite as had been instructed. 'Don't shoot humble self, excellent and honourable sir.'

'What's that you're holding?' Galsworthy demanded.

Although Tommy had created something of a diversion,

causing Galsworthy to take his pistol out of alignment on Ole Devil, there was no hope of it being turned to the trio's advantage. The Mexicans had brought up their weapons and we're covering the Texian.

'Don't shoot him!' Old Devil called urgently. 'It's only his *kongo*.'

'His *what*?' Galsworthy asked, refraining from squeezing the trigger as he saw the thing Tommy was holding and decided that it could do him no harm.

'A *kongo*, mister,' Ole Devil repeated. 'It's his *yawara* prayer stick.'

Laying across Tommy's left palm, the *kongo* looked harmless. It was a rod of some kind of hard wood, rounded at the ends and with grooves carved around its six inch length.

'If I am to join honourable ancestors,' Tommy went on, displaying the *kongo*. 'I must make *yawara* prayer.'

'We'll give you a chance to do it before we kill you, if you behave,' Galsworthy promised, grinning sardonically and dismissing both Tommy and the *kongo* as of no importance.

The handsome man considered that he had every right to feel satisfied with the way things had turned out. When Arnaldo Verde had first come to him for help, he had seen a way in which he might make a lot of money. Loyalty to the Mexican citizenship he had adopted was not his motive for serving Santa Anna. In fact, his were much the same motives that Ole Devil had given Grivaljo. Five hundred new caplock rifles and a plentiful supply of ammunition were very valuable commodities. They would command a high price whether sold in bulk or individually. He had no intention of turning them over to the Mexicans if they should fall into his hands. So, while he was willing to destroy the shipment if necessary, he had been determined to gain possession of it if possible.

With his band scattered, looting the properties which had already been deserted by their owners or pillaging such as were still occupied but only lightly defended, Galsworthy had lacked sufficient strength to attack the Brindleys and take over the means to transport the shipment. So, having sent Halford and four men with Verde to intercept General Houston's messenger, he had tried without success to gather reinforcements. Failing to do so, he had left word for any of his band who arrived at their headquarters to come after him and had taken the remainder, including his wife, to Gonzales. He had not known that the remnants of Halford's party were in the vicinity when he had visited the Brindleys' ranch to size up the opposition.

The meeting with Ole Devil had informed Galsworthy that Halford had failed in his assignment. When he had learned of Mucker's capture, he had known that he must not allow an interrogation to be carried out. Mucker was neither brave nor staunch and would talk. He had known too much to be left alive. So Galsworthy had excused himself and gone to the barn. Finding it deserted and the key in the storeroom's door, he had availed himself of the opportunity with which he was being presented. Entering, he had killed Mucker with his sword-cane. Having laid the body on the bed and covered it with a blanket, he had locked the door and rejoined his party.

Still determined to try and take the shipment, Galsworthy had realized that he could not hope to do so unless he had more men. So he had reduced the number of his already small party by dispatching one of them in search of other members of his band. Having done so, he had brought the rest to the coast. He had known that the mule train would have to come to Santa Cristobal Bay and had wanted to study its strength with the idea of taking it over. Instead of staying in sight of the Bay, he had taken his party to a hill which offered a good view of the surrounding country and had set a watch against the train's arrival.

Learning that Di was approaching accompanied by Ole Devil and Tommy much earlier than he had anticipated, Galsworthy had guessed that they were travelling a long way ahead of the mule train. He had also seen he was being given a chance to outwit them. With the girl in his hands, he could force her grandfather to transport the shipment and, as long as he held her hostage, he could ensure that there would be no trouble from the old man or the Tejas Indian mule-packers.

Knowing that Halford had been a better than fair fighting man, Galsworthy had acquired considerable respect for Ole Devil's capabilities in that line. Any man who could get by Halford – who had been with Galsworthy for several years and was second-in-command of the band – with the backing that he had was far too dangerous to be treated with anything other than great care. So, with Madeline's approval, Galsworthy had formulated a plan to get her into his potential victims' company. He had not been worried about asking his wife to take on the task. In spite of her elegant appearance and air of being a well-bred lady, she was tough, ruthless and able to take care of herself.* As long as her true purpose was not suspected, having her attached to the Texian's party would be a great advantage.

Realizing that there would be a certain amount of danger involved if they were to make the woman's 'rescue' appear genuine, the conspirators had planned it carefully. Although Galsworthy's warning had probably not been necessary, the Mexican 'captors' had been instructed to allow Madeline to 'escape' at some distance away from her 'rescuers' so as to lessen the chances of being shot by them. The precautions had been justified. However, due to the nature of the terrain, they had been nearer than they had intended before Di's hasty actions had allowed them to locate the trio and put the scheme into action.

On the other hand, Madeline's part of the plan had gone without a hitch. She was an excellent rider and had been mounted upon a well-trained horse which she had been confident she could trust. While she had been sitting side-saddle with her hands fastened behind her back, her bonds had been tied around the thick leather gauntlets. So, as an experiment had proved, she could have freed herself if necessary. As a further air, should she have needed to regain control of the black gelding, its reins were dangling across its neck and the Mexican was leading it by a rope that was too short to have entangled its legs when he had released it.

Everything had gone to plan. In fact, Madeline considered that her worst moment had been when Ole Devil had questioned her about the side-saddle. Fortunately, she had been sufficiently quick witted to have thought up a plausible excuse.

When Madeline had heard about the presence of the Mexican brig in the bay, she had recognized that it was posing a serious threat to her husband's hopes. It would either frighten away, or capture, the ship that was delivering the rifles. No matter

* Before their conduct had made the United States too hot to hold them and they had fled to Texas, Madeline and her husband – whose full name was Randolph Galsworthy Buttolph – had operated a high-class combined brothel and gambling house in New York. While there, Madeline had earned a well-deserved reputation for being able to quell – by physical means if necessary – the toughest and most recalcitrant of their female employees or competitors.

which happened, the consignment would be lost to them. Listening to her 'rescuers' discussing the situation, she had been faced with another dilemma. She was aware of Galsworthy's desire to capture and use the girl as a hostage. With that in mind, she had tried to talk Di out of accompanying the men. Discovering that the girl was adamant, Madeline had offered to participate in a more active manner than had been suggested. Although not entirely displeased at being refused – for she considered the chances of failure were high – she had been irritated by the way in which Di had turned down her suggestion. Clearly the girl had considered that she would be more of a liability than an asset on such a hazardous mission. Being proud of her reputation for competence and toughness, she had resented being treated that way by a poorly educated country yokel even though she should have regarded it as a tribute to her acting ability. However, she had managed to conceal her resentment and, apparently yielding to Di's greater experience, had even consented to the exchange of clothing.

Shortly before nightfall, having followed the tracks of his wife and her 'rescuers', Galsworthy had found his wife at the cabin. On being told why she was alone and dressed in such an outlandish fashion (although he had regarded the clothing as very fetching due to the way in which she filled them) he had expressed his approval of her actions.

Then, in case the attempt to get rid of the brig should be successful, Galsworthy and his wife had made plans to capture the trio on their return. Wanting to take them alive if possible and having heard nothing to diminish his regard for Ole Devil's abilities, Galsworthy had told his party what he wanted them to do. There were now only three men with him, the fourth having been sent back to look for and speed the arrival of such other members of the band whom he should meet.

Although Galsworthy had known that it would most likely be after dawn before his victims arrived, he had been disinclined to take chances. So, while he and his wife had spent the night making love in the cabin, their horses had been picketed beyond the nearest clump of bushes. The three very disgruntled men had been compelled to occupy a draughty and poorly constructed barn, being under orders to ensure that at least one of them remained awake and alert at all times.

Galsworthy had had no way of knowing how well, or otherwise, his order had been carried out. With his passions aroused by Madeline's sensual appearance, he had been too occupied in sating them to check up on the trio. Certainly he had not found any of them asleep, although all looked damp, depressed and miserable, when he visited them at the first hint of daybreak. The party had eaten a cold breakfast as he had refused to allow a fire to be lit in case their victims should see the smoke and become suspicious. After that, it had only been a question of waiting. One of the men had been sent to keep the horses hidden and quiet. The other two had been warned against letting themselves be seen before the Texian and his companions were disarmed.

There had been no doubt in Galsworthy's mind that the plan would succeed. A man of Ole Devil Hardin's background would do nothing to endanger the life of a woman, especially as she had apparently been helpful and was, as far as he knew, a loyal Texian.

The gamble had paid off. All that remained for Galsworthy to do was secure his prisoners and, provided they had done the work of removing the Mexican ship, await the arrival of the arms and the means to transport them.

[Note from page 147: The damage had gone unnoticed and unsuspected until late that afternoon. On running into a squall, the *Destructor* brig's violent motions had completed the work which had been done by Tommy Okasi's saw. First one of the carronades, then the others in rapid succession, broke free. Careering about the heeling deck, the angle of which had altered with sudden and unexpected speed as the weight upon it kept shifting, the guns created havoc and chaos. In addition to killing and injuring several members of the crew, one of them collided with and brought down the forward mast.

No fool, Lieutenant Givaljo realized that he had been tricked and drew fairly accurate conclusions as to why it had been done. However, in view of the fact that considerable damage had been inflicted upon the brig – not the least of which was the loss overboard of all the broadsides' armament – he had accepted that it would be impossible for him to return in the hope of intercepting the ship which he suspected the Texians were awaiting at Santa Cristobal Bay.

Being aware of what his fate would be when his superiors heard of what had happened, Grivaljo took the battered brig into a small, deserted bay on the coast of Texas under the pretence of making sufficient repairs to let them reach Matamoros. While the work was being carried out, he deserted and, later, surrendered to the garrison at a Texian town. On discovering that he had gone, the rest of the crew followed his example.]

CHAPTER SIXTEEN

YOU NEED A LESSON, MY GIRL

ANGER, resentment and annoyance at having fallen for the
trick that had been played by the woman whom she knew as
Madeline de Moreau, was boiling through Diamond-Hitch
Brindley. It grew rather than diminished as the girl was watching the woman walking confidently towards her. There was an
arrogant mockery and more than a hint of smug self-satisfac-
tion on Madeline's beautiful features that Di was finding particularly infuriating. However, having no wish to endanger the
lives of her two companions, the girl managed to hold her
temper in check.

On reaching the place where Ole Devil Hardin had tossed
the bowie knife and Manton pistol, Galsworthy halted with the
intention of picking them up. Having studied them while he
was approaching, he knew that each weapon was far too valuable to be allowed to fall into his men's hands. The rest of the
party stopped when he did and stood awaiting his instructions.
Instead of speaking, he thrust the uncocked pistol with which
he had 'threatened' his wife through his waist-band.

Measuring with his eyes the distance which was separating
him from his captors, Ole Devil accepted that it would be futile
to take any action at that moment. Although Galsworthy was
putting away his weapon and had not yet removed the sword
from its cane-sheath, the two Mexicans still held their flintlock
pistols in their hands. Before he could reach and tackle their
leader, unless something happened to divert their attention, one
or the other of them was sure to have thrown down on him. At
such a short range, it was highly unlikely that they both would
miss.

'The Mexican brig's gone, *hombre*, but we did what we
planned before it sailed,' Ole Devil warned, playing for time.
'Which means it won't be coming back. There's no way *you* can
take the ship when it arrives.'

'Seeing that I've got *you*, I don't even have to *try* to take it,' Galsworthy replied, so delighted by the success of his planning that he could not resist boasting. Respecting the young Texian as he did was such an unusual sensation that he wanted to impress the other in return. 'All I have to do is use the authorization Houston gave to you and the captain will hand over the consignment.'

'Like hell he will,' Ole Devil contradicted, with an air of complete assurance.

'Why not?' Galsworthy demanded, having no wish to fail because of some error in his thinking.

'My Uncle Marsden arranged the shipment and is coming with it,' Ole Devil explained, so convincingly that he might have been telling the full truth. 'He won't turn it over to anybody but *me*. Try thinking about that before you kill us.'

'Don't kill humble self, honourable and excellent gentleman!' Tommy Okasi wailed, throwing himself to his knees and closing the fingers of his right hand around the *kongo* stick.

Raising both hands above his head as if in supplication, the small Oriental shuffled forward on his knees and started to howl something in his native tongue.

'What the hell's he doing?' Galsworthy growled, straightening up without having retrieved either of the weapons on the ground. He eyed Tommy with contempt.

'Praying to his ancestors to protect him,' the Texian replied, raising his right hand slowly. Removing his hat, he laid it reverently across his chest and went on in Spanish, 'May the Good Lord forgive him for being a heathen.'

The gesture was so touching that one of the Mexicans, being religiously indoctrinated like so many of his race and creed, crossed himself with his left hand. He did not, however, turn his pistol from its alignment on the young Texian. Being either less impressed, or not so pious as his companion, the other Mexican continued to point his weapon in the small Oriental's direction.

Seeing the way Tommy was acting, Di might have felt disgusted if she had not recollected the things Ole Devil had told her about him. Remembering that he had willingly and without hesitation agreed to handle a potentially dangerous task aboard the brig – even though he had apparently failed in his purpose, she found his present cowardly behaviour puzzling.

Then enlightenment struck the girl!

With it came the realization that Tommy was only being partially successful in his deception. Although the Mexican whom he was approaching appeared to be amused by his 'terrified' grovelling, the pistol was still aiming straight at the centre of his chest. Before he could get close enough to do whatever he was planning, the man might become suspicious and squeeze the trigger.

What was needed, Di concluded, was something to distract the men's attention away from her friends.

The next question the girl decided was, how could she do it?

Turning her gaze along the line of her enemies, Di brought it back to Madeline. The woman was standing with her hands on her hips, and looking at Tommy with something between amusement and contempt. Becoming aware of the girl's eyes on her, she returned the scrutiny.

Having gained some considerable proficiency at playing poker, it being a favourite pastime of her grandfather and all their employees regardless of race, Di possessed a fair ability to read human emotions if they were shown. Taking in Madeline's obvious delight and pleasure over their predicament, the girl guessed what was causing it.

Although Di had thought nothing of it at the time, having had more important issues demanding her attention, she had sensed on the previous afternoon that – no matter how Madeline was reacting on the surface – there had been an undercurrent of animosity because Di had refused her assistance. The girl now realized what had brought it about. Clearly Madeline – who must be possessed of considerable courage, determination and confidence to have accepted her role in the fake rescue – had resented a much younger and far less worldly-wise member of her sex snubbing her. She was obviously incensed that Di believed she lacked the kind of qualities which would be required during the proposed deception of the Mexican naval officer.

The experienced and confident way in which the woman had put up her fists when Di appeared to be on the point of attacking her, taken with Galsworthy's comment that she had been fortunate not to have done so, suggested that Madeline might not be a pampered, delicate and well-bred lady. She could, in fact, be a whole heap tougher than the girl had anticipated. What was more, while she filled the borrowed garments a mite snugly, there was little or no flabby fat on her gorgeous body.

Watching Madeline's face all the time, Di gripped the lapels of the riding habit's jacket. With a sudden jerk that popped off the buttons, she peeled it from her and flung it on to the ground. Anger replaced the mockery on the woman's beautiful features. Nor did it diminish as Di unfastened and released the shirt. Letting the garment slide down, the girl stepped backwards from it. She stood clad in her hat, the borrowed blouse, a pair of men's red woollen combinations and her moccasins.

'Here,' Di said, as she kicked the riding habit contemptuously in its owner's direction. 'Now you get the hell out of my duds, you fat bladder of cow-shit, afore you bust 'em at the seams.'

'You lousy little bitch!' Madeline hissed. Then she became calmer and started to move forward. Clenching and lifting her fists, she went on with malicious delight, 'You need a lesson, my girl.'

Almost before the woman had finished speaking, while Galsworthy was opening his mouth to yell at her to keep back, Di went into action. However, although the girl passed in front of Ole Devil, neither she nor Madeline came between him and the Mexican who was covering him

Seeing the girl darting to meet her, Madeline eagerly and briefly savoured the thought of what she was going to do. She wished that she was wearing some of her rings, as they had been of considerable use in other brawls. Having removed and left them in her husband's possession, as an added 'proof' that she had been robbed by her 'captors', she had not replaced them in case they should be noticed before the Texian was disarmed, warning him of what was really happening. However, she did not doubt that she could give the girl a thorough thrashing without such artificial aids.

Preparing to throw a punch into the girl's belly when close enough Madeline was expecting Di's hands to grab for her hair. Such had almost invariably been the tactics used by other women with whom she had come into conflict and it had given her a decided advantage. So it was an unpleasant surprise when, instead of obliging, the girl rammed a left jab into Madeline's right breast. What was more, the blow was far from being a wildly-thrown, unscientific feminine swing. Directed with masculine precision, the hard knuckles came in contact with the ultra-sensitive region.

Despite being almost at the end of its flight, Di's punch still caused enough pain to turn Madeline's advance into a retreat. Going back a couple of steps, the woman caught her balance and, as the girl followed, whipped up her right leg in a kick. Once again, the girl demonstrated that she was far more skilled than any of Madeline's earlier opponents. Stabbing out her hands, she caught the rising ankle with the right and cupped the left under the calf. Giving a heaving, circular twist, she turned the woman to her right and heaved. Screeching in mingled anger and alarm, Madeline went down and rolled over twice before coming to a halt on her back. Eager to make the most of her advantage, Di went after the woman.

Guessing what the girl was planning to do when he saw her disrobing, Ole Devil was ready to take advantage of any situation that might arise. The chance did not come immediately. However, as Madeline was pitched by him and Di followed her, the Mexican swung his gaze to watch them. In doing so, he allowed the barrel of his pistol to turn to the left.

Instantly, the Texian acted as he had planned to do if Tommy had succeeded in creating a diversion. Taking advantage of the fact that his three male enemies were watching the women, he sent his hat skimming through the air. It struck the Mexican on the left in the face, arriving with sufficient force to bring a yelping profane word of protest. Going back an involuntary pace, his forefinger jerked at the pistol's trigger. In doing so, he inadvertently caused the barrel to resume its alignment on Ole Devil.

The hammer fell, with the muzzle pointing straight at the centre of the Texian's chest!

Hitting and tilting forward the frizzen, the flint caused sparks which fell into the priming pan!

Like Ole Devil, Tommy had been alert for any chance to turn the tables on their adversaries. Seeing that the man in front of him was turning his head to stare at Di and Madeline, he stopped his lamentations and brought down his hands. If his captors had been more observant, they might have noticed that he had ended his crawling with the left knee on the ground and the right leg bent. It was a posture which allowed rapidity of movement.

Even as Ole Devil threw the hat, Tommy thrust himself

erect and forward all in one movement. There was need for every bit of speed he could muster. Catching the movement from the corner of his eye, the Mexican was starting to return his attention to the small Oriental.

Reaching Madeline, it became Di's turn to grow over-confident. Standing on her right leg, she raised her left foot with the intention of stamping on the woman. While Madeline had been taken by surprise, she was a skilled rider and had learned how to reduce the force of even an unexpected fall. So she was far from being as helpless as the girl imagined.

Rolling on to her side, Madeline let the downwards-thrusting foot strike her right shoulder. She was hurt by doing so, but not as badly as she would have been if she had taken the attack on the bust or stomach. Ignoring the pain, she grabbed for and jerked Di's right leg from under her. Losing her hat as she landed, the girl proved to be just as capable at breaking a fall. However, before she could recover, the woman was on top of her and two strong hands closed around her throat.

Moving like lightning, Tommy used his left hand in a scooping, outwards motion to deflect his victim's – and, under the circumstances, there could be no other term for the Mexican – weapon. Having turned the pistol so that it was no longer a threat to his well-being, the small Oriental demonstrated the true purpose of the *kongo* – and proved in no uncertain fashion that it was anything but a harmless piece of wood used as an aid to prayer.

A *kongo* was, in fact, a deadly weapon when wielded by a student of *yawara*.*

Even as his left hand came into contact with the pistol, Tommy was twisting his upper body in the opposite direction to the way he was pushing the weapon. He raised his right arm outwards, bending the elbow and turning the hand so that the knuckles were uppermost. Then he pivoted his torso to the front

---

* The self-defence system known as *yawara* had its origins in Okinawa over a thousand years ago. Having been forbidden by the invaders who had conquered their home land to own or carry weapons of any kind, the Okinawans had developed and perfected the use of the innocuous-looking *kongo* stick which became known as the 'six inches of death' because of its lethal capabilities. It was so simple to manufacture that, if one had to be discarded for any reason, there would be no difficulty in replacing it. The *kongo's* small size made concealment easy and carrying had been no problem.

and snapped the right fist forward so that the rounded point*
of the *kongo* was carried towards its target.

The small Oriental's attack was delivered before its recipient
could even start to appreciate his terrible predicament. Nor was
he given a chance to try and avert it. Driving upwards with
speed and power, the *kongo*'s point ended its propulsion against
the *jinchu*; the collection of nerves which came together in the
centre of the top lip. Blood spurted as the wood ground into the
flesh and an unimaginable agony detonated through the Mexican. Everything seemed to disintegrate around him into a cata-
clysm of roaring flame. Slipping from his fingers, the pistol fell
to the ground.

From delivering the blow, Tommy let his hand continue to
rise until it was above his left shoulder. Once again he whipped
it forward. This time, it was the butt of the *kongo* that connected. There was a sharp crack as it impacted on the centre of
the man's forehead. Already being driven to the rear, he pitched
over on to his back. He would never rise again, dying of con-
cussion without regaining consciousness.

Leaping forward to tackle Galsworthy, Ole Devil saw the
hammer of the Mexican's pistol swinging around and was
aware of where its barrel was pointing. There was, he realized,
nothing that he could do to save himself.

When Madeline rolled on to her, Di reacted instinctively and
in a completely feminine manner. Even as the hands started to
tighten and the woman raised her head from the ground, the
girl's fingers sank deep into the brunette locks. It was not the
first time that Madeline had had her hair pulled, but never with
such strength and savage violence. Screeching a pain-filled protest, she felt as if the top of her skull was being torn off. She
reared back and released the girl's neck with the idea of grabbing the wrists to try and relieve the agony. Instantly Di un-
tangled the right hand, folded and struck out with it. Caught
on the nose, Madeline's head snapped back and blood flowed
from her nostrils. The girl gave a surging heave which toppled
the woman from the upper position and twisted to gain it herself. Straddling Madeline's waist with her knees, Di sat up and
started to assail the beautiful, anger and pain distorted, features
with fore and backhand slaps.

Ole Devil should have been killed only one thing saved his

* The end of the *kongo* which protruded from between the thumb
and forefinger was the 'point' and the other end, the 'butt'.

life. The basic and often fatal flow of the flintlock system.

Having been out in the cold, damp air, the powder in the priming pan failed to ignite. Letting out a startled exclamation, the Mexican stared down at his weapon. Then, allowing it to fall from his hand, he grabbed at the knife that was sheathed on the left side of his belt.

Furious at his wife for her behaviour, Galsworthy saw Ole Devil approaching. At the same moment, he became aware of the change that had come over Tommy. Snapping a quick glance to his right, he saw the little Oriental delivering the attack. Hearing the dead click of a pistol and its user's exclamation, he swung his gaze in the other direction. What he saw filled him with alarm and he guessed what had caused the weapon to misfire. In all probability, his own pistol would fail to function for the same reason.

Ignoring the weapon that was thrust into his belt and those which were just in front of him, Galsworthy sprang backwards. His actions were motivated by a desire to gain sufficient time to unsheath his sword from inside the cane. Even as he moved, he realized that he was committing an error in tactics. If he had stood his ground, he might have been able to prevent the Texian from arming himself. It was, however, too late to change his mind. So he gripped the cane, twisted and started to draw from it the shining, razor-sharp blade.

'Dodd!' Galsworthy bellowed as the sword was coming free. 'Dodd! Get here!'

Reaching his weapons, Ole Devil grabbed for the one which he felt was most suited to his needs. He had watched Galsworthy's hurried retreat and guessed what was the reason for it even before he saw the unsheathing of the sword. To his right, the Mexican was already moving forward and pulling out a knife. While the pistol was percussion-fired and relatively impervious to damp, it held only a single shot. So Ole Devil's right hand closed around the concave ivory handle of the bowie knife.

Plucking the weapon from the ground, with Galsworthy's yell ringing in his ears, Ole Devil swung it around and out to the right. Seeing the great knife rushing at him, the Mexican arched his stomach to the rear and, with his body bent like a bow, flung himself away from its arc. Nor was he a moment too soon. The convex curve of the blade's point barely missed him. Continuing to withdraw and sliding free his own weapon, which suddenly seemed very puny and fragile in comparison to that held by the Texian, he was relieved when his assailant did not favour him with any further attentions, but went straight by.

Without waiting to see if there was any response to his yell, Galsworthy hurled the empty cane so that it went spinning parallel to the ground and at the Texian's head. Still moving forward, Ole Devil threw up his left hand to knock the missile aside. Galsworthy sprang forward, going into an almost classical lunge which sent the point of his sword flashing towards the young man's stomach.

After taking two slaps in each direction, which had rocked her head from side to side, Madeline responded. She was being held down by the girl's weight and knew what to do about it. Leaving the left wrist, as she realized that all she was doing was adding to the pain its hand was inflicting on her hair, she sent her fingers to the girl's bust. Sinking like talons into the firm mounds under the flimsy cover of the woollen combinations, they crushed and squeezed. Shrieking, Di tried to jerk away. As the pressure upon her was relieved, Madeline tipped Di over and regained the upper position. She was not there for long. Using all her strength, Di contrived to reverse their roles. Tearing at hair, slapping, punching, scrabbling and gripping with their hands, they rolled along the ground oblivious of everything except their hatred for each other.

Taking no notice of the squealing of the embattled women, Ole Devil skidded to a stop. Like many young men of his class and generation, he had been a regular attendant at a *salle des armes*. Not only had he learned fencing with the sabre and *epee de combat*, but his instructions had included fighting with a bowie knife against a similar weapon or a sword. The training stood him in good stead at that moment. Swinging the knife around in a circular motion, he used the flat of the blade to strike and deflect the sword to his left. Once it was clear of him, he disengaged and attempted a backhand slash to his opponent's neck. Galsworthy's rapid stride to the rear saved him. The razor-sharp false edge hissed by and, as he was about to advance, the knife returned in a swing that would have laid its edge across his throat if he had begun to move. Stepping further back, almost involuntarily, he made a rapid cut across with the sword only to be thwarted by the Texian's equally swift withdrawal.

On the point of going to his leader's assistance, the Mexican became aware that Tommy was coming towards him. A glance at the bloody face of his companion, who was sprawled supine and motionless, gave a warning that the small Oriental might be far more dangerous than his earlier behaviour had suggested. However, as the Mexican held a knife and was skilled in its use, he did not feel particularly perturbed. He failed to notice the *kongo*. Even if he had seen it, having been watching the women when his *amigo* was attacked, he probably would not have appreciated its true purpose. Darting to meet Tommy, he put his faith in a low thrust that curved inwards towards the stomach.

Protecting himself with a backhand and downwards blow, Tommy miscalculated a little. His wrist struck the Mexican's forward driving forearm. While the knife was turned to his left and in front of him, the defence was less damaging than it would have been if it had been delivered by the rounded butt of the *kongo*. Instead of having his arm numbed, if not more seriously injured, the Mexican was able to snatch it clear of the small Oriental's wrist. Then he whipped the knife back and up in the direction of Tommy's throat.

Having heard the commotion, and also seeing something which had been a source of pleasure and satisfaction, the last member of Galsworthy's party ran from behind the clump of bushes which was being used to hide the horses. Taking in the sight a good hundred and fifty yards away, he cocked and whipped the rifle that he was carrying to his shoulder. At the same time, he gave advice and some news which he felt sure his leader would find most acceptable under the circumstances.

'Get clear of him, boss!' the man yelled, trying to line his weapon but not caring to attempt a shot at that distance with the Texian so near to Galsworthy. 'It's all right. Some of the boys're coming.'

CHAPTER SEVENTEEN

I'LL KILL YOU FOR THIS, HARDIN!

HEARING his man's yell, Galsworthy tried to do as he had been requested. However, Ole Devil Hardin had also heard and appreciated the danger. So, when Galsworthy leapt backwards, he followed and tried to crowd in closer. Even though retreating, Galsworthy continued to wield his sword defensively. The extra length of his enemy's blade forced the Texian to keep at a distance from which his bowie knife could not make contact. Yet, if the man was speaking the truth – and there did not appear to be any reason why he should lie – there was urgent need for Ole Devil to act quickly. He had to deal with Galsworthy, separate the fighting women and get his party into the shelter of the cabin before the reinforcements arrived.

Crouching swiftly, Tommy Okasi allowed the Mexican's knife to pass just above his head. Having done so, he lunged forward with his right arm. Rising rapidly, the point of the *kongo* took his assailant in the *solar plexus* with all the driving force of his muscular frame behind it. Such a blow was deadly in the extreme. Letting go of the knife, as the sudden onrush of pain caused paralysis and loss of consciousness, the man crumpled. He went down like a pole-axed steer and with just as permanent results.

Even as the Mexican was falling, Tommy sprang clear and turned his attention to his companions. Diamond-Hitch Brindley and Madeline de Moreau were rolling over and over, screeching like a pair of enraged bobcats. In a tangle of wildly thrashing and waving limbs. Deciding that they were the least of his worries at the moment, for he too had heard Dodd's shouted advice, he swung his gaze to where Galsworthy was trying to put it into effect.

Lining his rifle, Dodd saw what he felt would be his chance. Galsworthy had retired fast enough to put just sufficient distrance between him and the Texian for the man to be willing to act. His forefinger tightened on the trigger and, unlike the Mexican, he had contrived to keep the powder in his priming pan dry. So, after the inevitable brief delay while the priming charge ignited, reached and detonated the powder in the chamber, the rifle roared.

Hit in the upper part of the crown by Dodd's bullet, Ole Devil's hat was snatched from his head. While he realized what must have happened, the narrow escape caused him to duck involuntarily. Like a flash, Galsworthy turned his retreat into an attack. He saw that he had passed beyond the point where a lunge would serve his purpose. So, despite being aware of the basic flaw in its use, he went into a *flèche*. Bounding forward, he drove ahead with the sword at shoulder height and his torso leaning towards his potential victim.

With the needle-sharp point of the sword rushing in his direction, Ole Devil halted on spread apart feet and slightly bent knees. Just – and only just – in time, he swivelled himself at the hips and inclined his torso to the rear. As his assailant's weapon went by, its edge slicing a couple of the buckskin fringe's thongs from his shirt, he reversed his direction and the bowie knife swung in a glistening arc.

With a sickening sensation of horror, Galsworthy saw that his attack had failed. The worse feature of the *flèche* was that, if it did not succeed, the almost invariable result was a complete loss of balance and control from which, particularly against such an able opponent, there was no hope of recovery. So it proved. Carried onwards by the impetus of his movements, he watched the great knife passing under his sword arm. Then a sudden numbing sensation drove all coherent thought from his head. Biting in through his shirt, the blade sank deep and tore across his belly. There was a rush of blood and his intestines poured from the hideous wound as he stumbled by the Texian. Sinking to his knees, he toppled forward on to his face.

Having disposed of his attacker, Ole Devil straightened up and looked around. He found that Tommy had already succeeded in rendering the second Mexican *hors-de-combat*, which did not come as any surprise. However, the danger was far from over. The man whose bullet had nearly ended the fight in Galsworthy's favour had turned and was yelling for the group of about ten riders who were approaching to get a move on. Having seen and heard, Ole Devil swung his eyes to the two women.

'Grab my pistol, Tommy!' the Texian ordered, knowing that an extra weapon might be very useful. 'Then get Di into the cabin.'

'Can do!' the little Oriental answered as Ole Devil swung around and started to run to where their horses were standing.

Going forward, Tommy returned the *kongo* to his trousers' pocket. He picked up the Manton pistol and, guessing that he was going to need both hands to separate the women, thrust it through his waist belt. Waiting until Di came on top, he bent and catching her under the armpits, heaved. The girl let out a startled shriek as she felt herself plucked from her rival and sent staggering backwards. Sitting up, Madeline tried to rise. Before she could do so, Tommy delivered a *tegatana* chop to the top of her head. Stunned, she flopped limply on to her back.

Wild with rage, Di managed to keep on her feet and came to a stop. The blouse had gone and the combinations had been torn from her left shoulder, leaving that side of her torso bare to the waist. Oblivious of her appearance, she charged forward so as to resume the attack on her recumbent opponent.

Realizing that trying to reason with the girl in her present frame of mind would be a waste of time, Tommy made no attempt to do so. Darting to meet her, he caught her right wrist with his left hand as she tried to hit him. Bending forward, he thrust his other hand between her legs and, turning, jerked her across his shoulders. To the accompaniment of blistering invective from the furious girl, while her legs waved wildly and her free hand beat a tattoo on his back, he started to run towards the cabin. On entering, he dumped Di to the floor hard enough to jolt the wind out of her. Satisfied that he could leave her untended for the moment and hoping that, on recovering her breath, she would also come to her senses, he returned to the door. As he did so, he pulled out and cocked the pistol. From what he could hear, the weapon was likely to be needed in the near future.

Reaching his dun, Ole Devil slid the Browning rifle from its sheath with his left hand. Keeping the riders under observation, he noticed that one of them was better mounted than the rest and had already passed Dodd. Like his companions, who were coming as fast as they could manage, the leader had already drawn and cocked a pistol. Deciding to wait until he was indoors before loading the Browning, Ole Devil sprinted towards the cabin. As he was approaching the half-way point, he realized that the leading rider would have reached him before he could attain the safety of the building.

Seeing his employer's predicament, Tommy Okasi sprang outside. He swung up the Manton in both hands, sighted and fired. Struck in the chest by the bullet, the man slid sideways from his saddle. Slowing down to let the horse race by, Ole Devil increased his pace as it did so. Several shots were fired at him. With lead flying around him, he flung himself the last few feet. Stepping aside to let Ole Devil enter, Tommy followed him in and slammed the door.

Dropping the bowie knife, the Texian hurried to the nearest window. As he went, he reached behind him to pull a magazine bar from the pouch on the back of his belt. He eased it into the aperture, guiding it home and thumbing down the lever to seat it correctly. Then, drawing down the under-hammer, he thrust the barrel through the window to line it at the approaching men. Although he was aware that the pistol in his hand was empty, Tommy went to the other window and duplicated Ole Devil's actions.

Seeing the two weapons emerging and pointing in their direction, the remainder of Galsworthy's men veered away. While the pistol and the rifle held only a single shot each, or so they assumed in the latter's case, every man was aware that he had only one life. With that sobering thought in mind, not one of them was willing to press home the attack as he might become selected as a target. Instead, they galloped by the building, those who had not already done so firing in passing. The rest took in the sight of their companions who had already fallen to the defenders.

Galsworthy and the two Mexicans lay without movement, the former in an ever-growing pool of his own blood. Sitting up and feeling at her head, Madeline gazed about her dazedly. The buckskin shirt had come out of her borrowed trousers, which were now burst open along the seams. Her underclothing had been torn apart in the tussle, leaving her magnificent bosom exposed. Such a sight would have warranted the men's attention and study under less demanding circumstances, despite her once immaculate hair now resembling a woollen mop and her slap-reddened face being smeared by gore from her own and Di's bleeding noses. Sobbing as she fought to replenish her lungs, she started to rise.

In the cabin, the girl was also recovering. Gasping in air, she managed to get to her feet. For a moment she stood swaying and glaring about her as if ready to attack the first thing that moved. Then the wild light faded from her eyes as she realized where she was and, from her companions' positions at the windows, what must be happening outside. Ignoring the blood which was running out of her nostrils to splash from her chin on to her heaving and only partially covered breasts, she staggered to where her rifle was standing in the corner. Grabbing it up, she crossed to where Ole Devil was standing and cocked back the hammer as she went.

Standing up and swaying in exhaustion, Madeline had acted in much the same way as Di was doing in the building. Then she too became aware that the situation had changed. Staring around, her eyes came to rest on her husband's body. For a moment, she looked at the gory corpse. A shudder shook her and she swung away from it.

'I'll kill you for this, Hardin!' the woman shrieked, glaring and shaking her fists at the cabin.

Even if she had tried, Madeline could hardly have selected a worse – or – in one way, better – moment to make the threat. Even as she spoke, Di reached the window of the cabin. Before Ole Devil could stop her, the girl had lined the rifle and was squeezing its trigger. Although the weapon roared, Madeline was lucky. Still feeling the effects of being dropped on to the floor, Di was not controlling her breathing and caused the barrel of her rifle to waver up and down. So the bullet passed just over, instead of through, the woman's head. The narrow escape from death served as a warning to Madeline. Turning, she fled as fast as her exhausted condition would allow to where her men had halted their horses about a hundred and fifty yards from the building. One of them returned, guiding his mount around and, scooping her up, he carried her to their companions.

'Wh – What now?' Di gasped, lowering the rifle.

'Get loaded before they come at us,' Ole Devil answered. 'Tommy, string your bow. I'll try to keep them back while you're doing it.'

Holding the Browning ready for use while his orders were being carried out, the Texian watched the woman's rescuer set

169

her down by the rest of the men. They were recharging their pistols, but she started to order – or try to persuade – them to attack the cabin. Ole Devil guessed that they would take some action – although he doubted if it would be a frontal assault – once the weapons were ready.

Everything depended upon whether Di could reload her rifle and Tommy string the bow before the men had made their preparations. Even if they did, the odds were still in their assailants' favour.

Suddenly Dodd, who had joined his companions leading the woman's and dead men's horses, let out a yell and pointed to the west. Although Ole Devil could not see what had attracted his attention, clearly the other men found it a cause for alarm. Their horses milled as they stared in the direction Dodd had indicated and consternation reigned amongst them.

'Rush the house!' Madeline howled. 'You can do it before they get here!'

'Like hell we can!' a man answered and set his horse into motion. 'I'm going!'

Panic was always infectious. Given such guidance, the rest of the men followed their companion's example. Splitting up, they scattered in every direction except the west. Only Dodd remained, saying something urgently to the raging woman and pointing to the horse with two bed-rolls fastened to the cantle of its saddle. When she showed no sign of taking his advice, Dodd dropped the reins of the animals he was leading and sent his own mount bounding forward. The final desertion appeared to have a sobering effect on the woman. Going to the horse which the man had indicated, she hauled herself on to its saddle and followed him.

Puzzled by the departure, Ole Devil wondered if it might be a trick to lure his party into the open. Two minutes went by and, as Di joined him holding the reloaded rifle, he saw something that informed him there was no further danger from Madeline and her men.

On his return to the Texas Light Cavalry, Mannen Blaze had given Colonel Fog a report and a request from Ole Devil. The latter having been granted, Mannen had set off to join his cousin, accompanied by the whole of Company 'C'. Fifty strong, they had arrived in time to chase away their commanding officer's enemies.

Next day, just before noon, the ship glided into Santa

Cristobal Bay. Standing on the rim and watching the anchor go down, Ole Devil and Di exchanged glances. The girl had tidied up her appearance and donned clothes from her warbag. Apart from a black eye and swollen top lip, she showed no evidence of the fight. With his men tired from their long, hard ride, Ole Devil had not sent them after Madeline. He had doubted whether she would cause any more trouble.

Going down the slope towards the water's edge, young Ole Devil Hardin felt a sense of elation. The ship had brought the rifles. Now it was up to him to see that they reached General Houston.

THE END

If you have enjoyed reading this book and other works by the same author, why not join

THE J. T. EDSON APPRECIATION SOCIETY

You will receive a signed photograph of J. T. Edson, bi-monthly Newsletters giving details of all new books and re-prints of earlier titles.

Competitions with autographed prizes to be won in every issue of the Edson Newsletter.

A chance to meet J. T. Edson.

Send S.A.E. for details and membership form to:

The Secretary,
J. T. Edson Appreciation Society,
P.O. Box 13,
MELTON MOWBRAY,
Leics.

YOU'RE A TEXAS RANGER, ALVIN FOG
by J. T. EDSON

In every democracy the laws for the protection of the innocent allows loopholes through which the guilty can slip ... The Governor of Texas decided that only unconventional methods could cope with the malefactors who slipped through the meshes of the law and so was formed a select group of Texas Rangers. Picked for their courage, honesty, and devotion to justice, they were known as Company Z ...

With one exception every man in Company Z had been a member of the Texas Rangers for several years. Alvin Fog was that man. He had inherited the muscle, skill at gun handling and bare handed fighting of his grandfather, the legendary Rio Hondo wizard, Dusty Fog. But still his fellows in Company Z were not convinced he had the skill needed for their unconventional duties. It was up to him to prove he was worthy of his place in Company Z. He alone could make his fellow rangers say ... 'You're a Texas Ranger, Alvin Fog ...'

0 552 11177 5 - 75p

THE WHIP AND THE WARLANCE by J. T. EDSON

Having thwarted one scheme to invade Canada from the USA, Belle Boyd, the Rebel Spy, and the Remittance Kid were hunting the leaders of the plot, who had escaped and were plotting another attempt. To help them, they called upon a young lady called Miss Martha Jane Canary - better known as Calamity Jane ... Belle, Calamity and the Kid made a good team, but they knew they would need all their fighting skills when the showdown came. For they faced leLoup Garou and the Jan-Dark, the legendary warrior maid with the warlance who, it had long been promised, would come to rally all the Indian nations and drive the white man from Canada.

0 552 10964 9 - 65p

OLE DEVIL AT SAN JACINTO by J. T. EDSON

In 1835, the oppressions of President Antonio Lopez de Santa Anna had driven the colonists in Texas to rebellion. Major General Sam Houston, realizing that his small force could only hope to face the vast Mexican army when conditions were favourable, had ordered a tactical withdrawal to the east.

At last, on Thursday, April 21st, 1836, Houston decided that the time had come to make a stand. The Mexican Army, fifteen hundred strong, was on the banks of the San Jacinto river: Houston, with half that number, launched the attack that would decide the future of Texas.

0 552 10505 8 - 60p

SHANE by JACK SCHAEFER

'CALL ME SHANE.' He rode into our valley in the summer of '89 a slim man dressed in black, riding easily. He never told us more than his name.

'There's something about him,' Mother said, 'something . . . dangerous.'

'He's dangerous all right,' Father replied, 'but not to us.'

'He's like a slow-burning fuse,' the mule skinner said. 'So quiet, you forget it's burning till it sets off trouble. And there's trouble brewing . . .' There was.

One of the greatest novels ever to come out of the American West.

0 552 10968 1 - 65p

SUDDEN by OLIVER STRANGE

A trio of land-grabbing brothers . . . a crooked town marshal . . . a beautiful woman . . . between them, they had the town under their heel. Now they meant to take the whole range, their weapons terror and destruction and murder.

Into this Arizona hell-town the Governor sent Sudden. His instructions were brief: 'Clean it up', he said. 'No loose ends'. One man. A Texas outlaw with a badge. Sudden.

0 552 11797 8 - 95p

SUDDEN: APACHE FIGHTER by OLIVER STRANGE

The Apaches were massing in the mountains, and talking of a big war to sweep the hated white-eyes out of their land for all time. Bounty hunters stoked the fires of hatred with every warrior they ambushed. Apacheria was like a powder-barrel waiting for a spark. Into it, on a long chance, Governor Bleke sent the one man he could trust. A man not afraid to face the Apaches on their own ground, with their own weapons. A man they called - Sudden.

0 552 11800 1 - 95p

A SELECTED LIST OF CORGI WESTERNS

WHILE EVERY EFFORT IS MADE TO KEEP PRICES LOW, IT IS SOME-TIMES NECESSARY TO INCREASE PRICES AT SHORT NOTICE. CORGI BOOKS RESERVE THE RIGHT TO SHOW AND CHARGE NEW RETAIL PRICES ON COVERS WHICH MAY DIFFER FROM THOSE ADVERTISED IN THE TEXT OR ELSEWHERE.

THE PRICES SHOWN BELOW WERE CORRECT AT THE TIME OF GOING TO PRESS (MARCH '81).

J. T. EDSON:

☐ 08194 9	CUCHILO No. 43		95p
☐ 08012 8	SAGEBRUSH SLEUTH No. 24		95p
☐ 08018 7	TERROR VALLEY No. 27		95p
☐ 08132 9	THE SMALL TEXAN No. 36		95p
☐ 07900 6	McGRAW'S INHERITANCE No. 17		95p
☐ 07963 4	RANGELAND HERCULES No. 20		95p

LOUIS L'AMOUR:

☐ 08673 8	NORTH TO THE RAILS		95p
☐ 09342 4	BRIONNE		95p
☐ 09351 3	CONAGHER		95p
☐ 08157 4	FALLON		95p

OLIVER STRANGE:

☐ 11796 X	SUDDEN OUTLAWED		95p
☐ 11797 8	SUDDEN		95p
☐ 11799 4	SUDDEN AT BAY		95p

JOHN J. McLAGLEN:

☐ 10788 3	HERNE THE HUNTER 8: CROSS-DRAW		60p
☐ 10834 0	HERNE THE HUNTER 9: MASSACRE!		65p
☐ 11312 3	HERNE THE HUNTER 13: BILLY THE KID		85p

JAMES W. MARVIN:

☐ 11331 X	CROW 3: TEARS OF BLOOD		75p
☐ 11218 6	CROW 2: WORSE THAN DEATH		75p

All these books are available at your bookshop or newsagent ; or can be ordered direct from the publisher. Just tick the titles you want and fill in the form below.

CORGI BOOKS, Cash Sales Department, P.O. Box 11, Falmouth, Cornwall.

Please send cheque or postal order, no currency.

Please allow cost of book(s) plus the following for postage and packing.

U.K. CUSTOMERS. 40p for the first book, 18p for the second book and 13p for each additional book ordered, to a maximum charge of £1.49.

B.F.P.O. & EIRE. Please allow 40p for the first book, 18p for the second book plus 13p per copy for the next three books, thereafter 7p per book.

OVERSEAS CUSTOMERS. Please allow 60p for the first book plus 18p per copy for each additional book.

NAME (block letters) ....

ADDRESS ....

(MARCH 1981)..